Ribbons and Beaus

A Chaparral Hearts Novella

Kathleen Denly

RIBBONS AND BEAUS

First edition. January 1, 2020.

Copyright © 2020 by Kathleen Denly.

The characters and events in this fictional work are the product of the author's imagination. Any resemblance to actual people, living or dead, is coincidental.

Unless otherwise indicated, all Scripture quotations are taken from the Holy Bible, King James version.

Cover design by: Carpe Librum Book Design

Chaparral Hearts Series Order

Chronological:

Ribbons and Beaus (prequel novella ~ 1832-1834)
Waltz in the Wilderness (book 1 ~ 1854)
Cakes and Kisses (interquel novella ~ 1854)
Sing in the Sunlight (book 2 ~ 1858)
Harmony on the Horizon (book 3 ~ 1865)
Murmur in the Mud Caves (book 4 ~ 1873)
Shoot at the Sunset (book 5 ~ 1874)
TBA (book 6 ~ 1875)

Release Date:

Ribbons and Beaus (prequel novella) Released Jan 4, 2020
Waltz in the Wilderness (book 1) Released Feb 4, 2020
Sing in the Sunlight (book 2) Released March 2, 2021
Harmony on the Horizon (book 3) Released Jan 4, 2022
Cakes and Kisses (interquel novella) Released Dec 1, 2022
Murmur in the Mud Caves (book 4) Coming May 16, 2023!
Shoot at the Sunset (book 5) Coming 2024
TBA (book 6) Coming 2025

Dedication

To my Grandma Judi,
For always using different voices for the characters when she read me
bedtime stories, and for introducing me to the Christian historical
romance genre.

Psalm 139:14

I will praise thee for I am fearfully
and wonderfully made:
Marvellous are thy works;
And *that* my would knoweth right well.

Chapter 1
August 12, 1832

Millsworth, Ohio

Please don't let her be home. Jim Brooks hurried through the gentle rain along the path to the Taylors' back door. He lifted his hand to knock, then hesitated.

When Mr. Taylor had offered Jim the job of painting the Taylors' fancy front parlor, Jim almost turned the banker down. Then he'd remembered First Tuesdays. Nearly all the women hereabouts met at the church every first Tuesday of the month to spend the day gabbing and maybe adding a stitch or two to whatever quilt they was working on. According to his ma, Nora Taylor never missed a quilting bee.

Unless it were raining.

Jim glared up at the warm, late-summer rain and received a drop in the eye for his troubles. He rubbed the sting away and glanced back the way he'd come. Maybe he ought to go home, tell Mr. Taylor something came up. Jim could do the job some other day. Any day the man's daughter weren't around. Jim shook his head. No, that wouldn't do. He'd promised Mr. Taylor he'd do the job today. Jim may not be the sharpest scythe in the toolshed, but if he said it'd get done, it got done.

Sucking in a deep breath, he squared his shoulders, knocked on the door, and waited.

The persistent rain drummed against the top of his wool felt hat. Water plopped into a bucket left beside the back door. Several minutes passed, with Jim growing wetter by the second. But no tapping of a maid's shoes sounded across the Taylors' wood floor.

Well, I tried. Jim pivoted away.

Then he turned back. Set his jaw. He'd given his word and he weren't no coward. He knocked again, harder this time.

Still, no sounds came from within.

Side-stepping to the window beside the door, Jim cupped his hands against the glass and peered in.

Nothing but calico curtains.

Before Jim could pull away, the fabric drew back to reveal a pair of wide brown eyes over pink lips pursed in surprise.

Jim jumped back. *She's here.*

The curtain fell and the door swung open.

The most beautiful woman he'd ever laid eyes on stared back at him.

"Jim!" A delighted smile revealed her dimples—nearly the only thing about her that hadn't changed. "I didn't know you were coming." Her brows knit together and she glanced over her shoulder, then back to him. "Why are you knocking at the back door?"

Jim worked his mouth but no words would come.

Nora Taylor had always been prettier than a chicory bloom, but she'd only been gone six months, visiting her aunt in Boston. The breath-stealing, fancified woman before him couldn't be the same pest who'd nagged at his heels all these years while he collected rabbits from the traps her father let him set on the Taylors' land. It just weren't possible.

He rubbed the back of his wrist against his eyelids. He'd had the same argument with himself repeatedly in the two days that had passed since he'd seen her in town.

Unfortunately, it didn't change the facts. Little Nora Taylor *had* changed. He weren't the only man in town to have noticed either. He cleared his throat. "Your...uh...your father hired me to paint your parlor."

"Oh?" She looked past him to where he'd parked the wagon filled with supplies. "Then...you'll be here all day?"

Was that hope or dismay in her gaze? Jim ground his teeth. *It don't matter.* His little brother, Henry, had decided to court Nora the moment he spotted her stepping off the stage last week. Jim didn't even know Nora was back until his little brother raced into the yard, threw himself off his horse, and announced that he was going to marry Nora Taylor.

And that were that. Jim wasn't going to step in his little brother's way. No matter how pretty the picture before him.

"Oh! Where are my manners? Please, come in out of the rain." She pulled the door wide and stepped back.

Jim shook his head. "Got to get my supplies."

"Let me help!" Without waiting for a response, she darted past him into the summer shower.

Reaching the back of the wagon, she lifted the oiled canvas he'd used to protect his supplies from the weather, her arms stretched above her head. The pose showed off her strictly feminine curves.

My, but she made a striking figure.

How had he missed it? A body didn't change all that much in just six months, but try as he might, he couldn't recall ever noticing Nora Taylor had gone and growed up. Still, there weren't no denying that a woman, not a girl, was poking her nose into his supplies.

As he crossed the yard to join her, rain darkened the blue-and-cream-striped cotton fabric of her bodice.

Jim blinked and shook his head, dragging his gaze to the muddy path. *What are you doing? She's as good as Henry's wife.*

No matter that Jim's heart near-about stopped when he'd seen her himself the day after Henry's declaration, stepping out of the milliner's shop beside her mother. No matter that her brilliant smile had wrapped around him as warmly as a hug, nor that he'd not been able to look away from the curious spark in her eye as she invited him to supper. Thank the good Lord that Jim had already promised to eat supper with the pastor and his wife, or he might have accepted.

Even if Henry hadn't staked his claim, Jim weren't fool enough to chase after a woman too good for him. And Nora Taylor was far too good for him in ways that had nothing to do with her appearance.

Still, the temptation were strong. So he'd done everything he could to avoid her. But now here he stood, well and truly trapped into spending the day with her.

Or perhaps not.

He ran his sleeve across his forehead. "Were you planning on heading out? The paint's bound to smell something awful, and with the rain"—he shrugged—"you can't open the windows."

She tipped her face to the skies, heedless of the way the rain plastered her brown curls to her cheeks. "Oh, I don't think the rain will last much longer. Look."

He followed her pointing finger, and sure enough, a sliver of blue along the horizon promised a swift end to the unexpected rainfall. Stupid weather. Couldn't it make up its mind? "Still, the smell—"

"I don't mind." She started tugging one of the pigment-filled leather bags toward the end of the wagon. "What's in here?"

"Here." Jim rushed forward to grab it from her. "Let me get that. You should get back inside, out of the rain."

"Nonsense. I'm not sugar. I won't melt." She took it back from him. "Besides, if I help, it'll go faster. In fact, if you have an extra brush, I can help you paint, too." Hugging the large bag to her chest, she hunched over it to protect it from the rain as she scurried toward the house.

Jim lifted his eyes to heaven. "A little help?"

Another drop stung his eye.

Nora paused in the middle of the front parlor to survey its atypical chaos. It had taken only minutes for her and Jim to move his supplies from the wagon to her mother's favorite room and seconds longer to shove every scrap of furniture to the center of the room. Perhaps there was good to be found in the headaches that restricted Mother to her bed on days like today when the weather shifted so swiftly. She would be appalled by the transformation. Every one of the items Mother had added to enhance the beauty of this space was hidden beneath a layer of drab, stained canvas. In their place, sat a crate of rags, a battered box of tools and brushes, leather bags of pigments, a barrel of linseed oil, a tin of turpentine, and a...bag of chicken feathers?

She plucked one from its pouch. "What's this for?"

Jim snatched the feather from her hand and their fingers brushed.

Jim's eyes widened before he turned away and stuffed the feather back into the bag. "It's for the mahogany graining your father asked that I add to your woodwork." He finished stuffing the feather away and straightened, but didn't turn.

"So? What do we do?"

Jim ran a hand through his hair. "You really shouldn't be in here. The smell—"

"I already told you, I can handle the smell." She stepped around him and waved to the walls. "So? What's first?" For one heart-stretching moment of silence, Nora was certain he was going to order her from the room as her father would. She stepped toward him, tilting her chin way up to stare into his deep brown eyes. She forced a light-hearted teasing tone into her voice. "What's the problem, Jim? Worried I'll be better than you at this, too?" She poked his chest as she'd done dozens of times before when she'd challenged him to climb a tree faster, balance the fattest stick on his nose, or stare the longest without blinking. A zing traveled from her fingertip and along her arm. Touching him had been doing that to her for months before she'd left for Boston, but he'd never seemed to notice. He still saw her as the pesky little girl who followed him around, pestering him with questions and pointless challenges while he worked. Maybe challenging him had been the wrong tactic.

Instead of squaring his wide shoulders and puffing his chest as he used to, Jim wrapped his large, calloused fingers around the hand still poking him. "You've always been better than me. In every way." Releasing her, he spun away.

Wait. What does that mean?

He snatched a rag from the crate and tossed it at her. "Here."

She barely managed to keep it from smacking her in the face. "What's this for?"

"First thing we need to do is wash the walls." He eyed her head to toe. "You'd better change. Wouldn't want to ruin your fancy new dress."

She looked down at the tailored gown her aunt had purchased for her in Boston. It was the height of fashion and fit well in that bustling city. In Millsworth, it made as much sense as tying silk bows on a sow, but her mother insisted Nora continue dressing and acting the fine lady she wished Nora to be. She sighed. Her mother *would* be insufferable if Nora ruined the gown. "I'll be right back."

Two hours later, Jim gave the bucket of paint one final stir to be sure the pigment, oil, and turpentine were mixed thoroughly. Straightening, he looked over the freshly dusted walls. He'd assumed working with Nora would be the next thing to torture, but after returning in a serviceable brown dress, she kept to the wall opposite of wherever he was working. The two of them rotated like hands on a clock. She kept up a steady stream of chatter too, barely requiring a response from him. It was certainly a change from the days when she'd questioned him on everything under the sun.

He'd never understood why she did that. She was the top monitor in the town's school until she graduated from its highest level a little more than two years ago. Meanwhile, he spent his youth working alongside his pa as a chimney sweep, helping keep food on their table back east. Jim's mother mourned his lack of education, but by the time Pa died and she'd married Otis Davidson—who'd moved them to Ohio and *could* afford to send Jim and his little sister, Amanda, to school—Jim was no longer interested. At age eight, surrounding himself with a bunch of six-year-olds who knew twice as much as he did sounded about as much fun as being tarred and feathered. No thanks.

He steered clear of anyone his own age that had had more schooling than him. When the Taylors moved to town six years later, little Nora became his only exception. Mostly because he couldn't avoid her if he wanted to catch rabbits on her father's land. Despite being eight years his junior, six-year-old Nora already had a better education than his. Time had only expanded the gap. He'd often wondered why she bothered asking him questions when she was the one with all the book learning.

Now the questions seemed to be at an end.

She must've finally realized there wasn't much he could tell her that she didn't already know or couldn't figure out herself. It was only natural. In fact, it was something strange that it had taken her this long to recognize it.

So why did the lack of questions grate on him like the sandpaper he'd just used to prepare the wooden mantel?

Footsteps sounded in the hallway, interrupting his thoughts.

Nora must have finished rinsing the rags and hanging them to dry. The rain had appeared to stop just as they finished washing the walls, but gray clouds still darkened the sky so she'd decided to hang the rags in the kitchen. It was good she was headed back, though. They needed to get started, now that the paint was ready. He lifted the wooden lid from his toolbox and withdrew two round brushes. Painting would go twice as fast with Nora's capable hands to assist him. They'd not painted together before, but he'd yet to find anything she couldn't do well.

"Who are you?"

Jim spun toward the door.

Nora's mother leaned against the doorframe, her eyes narrowed.

Chapter 2

"Mrs. Taylor?" Jim dropped the brushes into the box. Hadn't her husband told her Jim would be working here today? "Was there something you needed, ma'am?"

A pained look on her face, Mrs. Taylor squinted in his direction. "Oh, Mr. Brooks." Mrs. Taylor let her eyes close and pinched the bridge of her nose. "I'd quite forgotten you were to come today. I came down to discover the source of that appalling odor." She cracked one eye to glare at the bucket of paint. "I suppose I've found it."

The windows! Jim hurried to open all three of the large parlor's windows before returning to stand before Mrs. Taylor. "I'm sorry, ma'am. I should've opened those as soon as the rain stopped. They're open now, so the smell should get better."

"Yes, well—"

"Mother!" Nora's voice sounded in the hall, and in a moment she was beside her mother. "What are you doing out of bed?"

"It's my fault, I'm afraid." Jim cringed. "Forgot to open the windows before I mixed the paint. Your mother was wondering about the smell." He resisted the urge to kick something. *What an idiot I am!*

"Well—" Nora took her mother's arm "—now that we've got that solved, shall I help you back to bed?"

"Yes." Mrs. Taylor let her daughter lead her away, but jolted to a stop at the base of their elegant staircase. "Wait!" She turned toward Jim, still watching them through the open parlor door. "My husband instructed me to ask you to leave a note on his desk informing him of the cost for the supplies as well as your labor."

Jim fought to keep the alarm from his expression. Write it down? He'd assumed he would simply tell Mr. Taylor what was owed as Jim had always done before, and that not until the job was completed. He'd bought his Ma's paint supplies at the same time as the Taylors' and the grocer had only told him the total amount. Jim had been counting on Henry looking over the grocer's notes to figure what amount Jim needed to charge Mr. Taylor and what amount Jim's family needed to pay.

He must have let some part of his distress show, since Mrs. Taylor added, "There are writing things on his desk as well. You may use those. Nora will show you where it is." Without waiting for a response, the two women continued up the stairs.

Jim stood in Mr. Taylor's fine study, his hands shaking as he stared at the grocer's notes. Jim hadn't needed Nora to show him the room. He'd been there a time or two before to speak with Nora's father. And Jim surely didn't want her staring over his shoulder while he tried to read. Were that a two or a five? He was always getting those two mixed up. His trembling blurred the already-messy handwriting. Ma had told him a dozen times to ask the grocer to write more neatly—neat handwriting made things easier on Jim when he did have to read—but Jim saw no call to slow the man at his work just because Jim was a dunce. Still, he should have asked the man to write two slips—one for the Taylor family and one for Jim's. But it hadn't seemed needed when he could just take it home for Henry to figure.

He braced his hand against the top of the desk and squinted at the numbers trotting down the right-hand side. That first one was a two. He was sure of it. Mostly.

With a growl, he crumpled the paper in his fist. Why was he so stupid? He hurled the balled-up paper at the door just as it opened.

It struck Nora square between the eyes.

She blinked, frozen in the doorway.

Regret rolled over him. Of all the times to lose his temper. "Sorry." He strode over to retrieve the wadded paper, but she beat him to it.

"What's this?" She smoothed the paper against her skirt. "Oh." She lifted her eyes to his, brows raised. "Trouble?"

"No." Jim's response came too fast, too sharp, too loud. He tried to snatch the paper from her grasp, but she was too quick.

Nora yanked the paper out of reach, did a little spin that sent her brown skirt whirling, and somehow ended up behind her father's desk. "You know, I can handle this. There's no need—"

"I can do it." Why was he arguing with her? They both knew it would take him ten times as long as it would for her to figure the amount their family owed.

She scrunched her face at him as she did whenever she was annoyed. "I was going to say, there's no need to let the paint you've already mixed go to waste."

The paint! He'd forgotten all about the paint waiting for him in the bucket. Would it need more turpentine now? "Just leave that there." He pointed to the desk. "I'll come back and write the note later."

"Don't be silly. I'll take care of this. You go get started on the painting."

He opened his mouth to protest, but she jabbed a finger at him.

"Aren't you the one always saying that dividing the work makes it go faster?"

He'd said that once, years ago, when he'd been desperate for a moment of quiet and thought if he could send her off to check traps on another part of the property, he might find some peace. "I don't always say—"

"And won't your mother be glad to have you home sooner rather than later?"

Nora did not play fair. She knew very well his Ma hated it when he missed supper—which he was likely to do if he hung around after the work was finished to try to figure that sum for the Taylors. "Fine." He spun on his heel and strode toward the door. "You rest here while I go do the *real* work."

In less time than Jim wanted to admit, Nora rejoined him in the front parlor. He braced himself for a deserved tongue-lashing—it'd been pure nonsense accusing her of resting—but she didn't speak. She just picked up the round brush, dipped it in the blue paint, and started working on the opposite wall.

Well then.

Jim returned to painting. She must have forgiven him already. That was kind of her. Then again, she did know him better than anybody. She must know he was sorry for being churlish.

The silence continued.

Jim waited for Nora to start talking. That woman weren't ever silent.

But the silence stretched so long, Jim thought his skin might bust open like a sausage over fire. Had Boston changed her so much? What was she thinking? Maybe she *hadn't* forgiven him. But if she were still mad, what was she doing helping him paint?

He glanced over his shoulder to where she'd nearly finished the last wall. Her shoulders were tight, her movements stiff.

Okay, so she was still mad.

He crossed the room to paint the upper portion of the wall she couldn't reach.

She didn't so much as blink. Just kept right on running her brush over the wall. Dip and stroke, stroke, stroke. Dip and stroke.

Like he weren't even there.

How could he apologize when she wouldn't even look at him?

"Nora?"

She kept on painting as if she couldn't hear him.

Hmph. Well, she could have it her way, then. Ignoring her, he focused on finishing the job he'd been hired to do.

He'd nearly reached the end of the wall a few minutes later when he bumped into something soft.

Nora squawked. "Hey!"

Arm still raised, he looked down to find Nora wedged between him and the corner. "Oh, sorry." The smell of her lilac soap drifted up to him.

Plop.

A fat drop of blue paint landed on her beautifully braided bun.

Her eyes widened as her mouth gaped open.

"Oh no!" He tried to wipe it away but the paint on his hands only made it worse. His fingers tangled in the braided knot on top of her head, dislodging several pins. Paint-smudged braids tumbled down around her shoulders. He tried to catch them and pile them back on top of her head.

"Here. I can fix it. I just..." His gaze searched the ground for the lost pins. There they were. But how to reach them without letting her hair loose again?

Her hair.

He was holding it.

He dropped her curls as if they'd singed him.

Nora batted her braids behind her shoulders, her gaze glued to Jim's face. What was he thinking? Clearly, he was horrified by the mess he'd caused. But there were more emotions flitting around in those deep brown eyes of his. *And* he'd stroked one of her braids with his thumb for the briefest of moments before releasing her hair.

She was sure of it.

Mostly.

Oh, why couldn't she just ask him how he felt about her? She'd asked him nearly every other question that had popped into her mind for years. Until one day last year, when he'd saved her from that tipping ladder. The feel of his arms around her sent a strange sort of warmth whizzing through her middle and popped into her consciousness the only question she didn't have the courage to ask. For the last year, it had remained trapped in her mind, unable to emerge. She'd tried. A few times. But just when she thought she'd worked up the nerve, her throat would tighten and she couldn't squeeze the words out.

Just thinking about asking him now caused tension in her neck. She rubbed it, encountering something wet.

Pulling her eyes from Jim, she examined her hand. Streaks of blue paint coated her fingertips. "Guess I'd better go wash."

Jim nodded, his Adam's apple bobbing as he swallowed.

Insufferable man. Couldn't he at least use proper manners? What had happened to his voice? It was certainly working when he made that remark about her resting while he worked. Not that she'd taken it personally. She knew it hurt his pride that she was better at reading, writing, and arithmetic. But what was she supposed to do? Stand around like an ornamental statue while he struggled for ages to complete something she could do in seconds? Would that truly be better?

She turned on her heel with a sigh and left the room. When she'd returned to the parlor, she decided not to speak until he spoke so that he'd have the advantage of choosing the topic. Her aunt had taught her that men liked to do the choosing and women should strive to agree with them as much as possible.

Nora wasn't sure Jim would agree with that last part—he seemed to enjoy their lively debates. But allowing him to choose gave him the advantage of conversing on a topic in which he was comfortable.

Except he didn't choose.

He'd worked in silence as though no one else was in the room. The longer he ignored her, the more frustrated she became. By the time he deigned to cross the room and attempt to engage her attention, she hadn't trusted herself to speak.

She flung open the back door, stalked across the puddle-speckled yard to the well, and wrapped her fingers around the crank. At least the rain had stopped.

"Let me."

Nora startled as Jim's large hand reached past her. His callused fingers brushed hers as she pulled her hand free, allowing him to take over lowering the bucket.

Trapped between the well and his body, the heat of his nearness warmed her back. It was tempting to lean into him. She stiffened. What was she thinking?

"I'm sorry, Nora."

She cleared her throat. "For what?"

"Your hair, and—"

"Oh, that was an accident. No need to apologize."

"And for what I said about you resting. I—" He shifted behind her.

She pivoted to look up at him.

He was close. Very close.

If he leaned down just an inch or two...

Her heels began to rise.

Nora lurched back, bumping into the side of the well. She teetered over the opening.

He caught her arms, steadying her.

How humiliating. She ought to look away. Heat seared her cheeks. She must appear as scarlet as Father's sealing wax. Yet she couldn't look away. "You saved me. Thank you." What *was* that look in his eyes?

"You're welcome." His voice was husky.

And he didn't let her go.

His fingers stroked her arms through her sleeves. "Nora, I..."

"Yes, Jim?" She couldn't help leaning toward him. He'd never looked at her like this before. Could it be? Was the intensity in his gaze attraction? Was he finally seeing her for the woman she'd become?

The clop and rattle of a carriage pulling onto her family's cobblestone front drive broke the tension. Her father had had the stones installed as yet another way to declare his family's station as higher than that of his neighbors and clients. He reveled in announcing his departures and returns each day with the clatter of hooves against stone.

Nora resented its disruption of the peace.

And now it had stolen this moment.

Chapter 3

Nora stood from her dressing table, patting her freshly coiffed hair. "Thank you, Mary. You're a dear."

Nora's lady's maid dipped a curtsy. "My pleasure, miss."

Rushing from the room and down the stairs, Nora prayed her father wasn't cross about her delay.

As their butler, Bertram, had passed the well on his way to the carriage house, he'd informed Nora that her father wished to speak with her in his study, but she couldn't appear before Father covered in paint. So she promised Jim that she would return to helping him as soon as she cleaned up and spoke with Father. Jim quietly responded that her help, though kind, was unnecessary. He'd insisted the job was easier accomplished alone.

Stubborn, confusing, frustrating man. Had he felt nothing in that moment by the well? Had she entirely imagined that Jim had been about to kiss her?

Pressing her fingers against her hot cheeks, she paused outside Father's study to collect herself. Deep breath in. Deep breath out. Once more. Raising her hand, she knocked on the door.

"Come in." His muffled voice sounded distracted, hurried. Had he even glanced up from the papers on his desk?

Irritation threatened. Deep breath in. Deep breath out. She opened the door and glided into the room, using the measured gait her mother had drilled into her.

With a calm expression that declared she had nothing of import with which to concern herself—as no lady ought to have any serious concerns—she stopped before her father, who was, indeed, bent over a ledger spread wide atop his desk. "You wished to speak with me, Father?"

Without glancing at her, nor moving his gaze from the column of figures before him, he snatched a small sheet of paper from beside the ledger and lifted it toward her. "What is this?"

"Mr. Brooks's invoice for the painting you hired him to do."

Impatience colored his words as he finally looked at her. "Yes, but why is it in your handwriting?"

"Well, I..." Her cheeks colored. "He was so busy, I offered to take care of this for him."

"You mean, he was too stupid to fulfill my simple request himself." He tossed the bit of paper to the desk with a look of disgust.

Fire roared to life inside her. "He is not stupid. He—"

"—is an uneducated man with no money, no connections, and no future worth discussing." Father's shoulders straightened, a hard glint in his eye. "And you spend far too much time with him. It was one thing when you were both children, but you are grown now and it must stop."

"I—"

Her father waved away her protest. "I am well aware of your infatuation with Jim Brooks. Do not try to deny it. But do know that I will not have it." He sighed and leaned back in his large, brown leather chair. "I'll grant you he *is* kind, honest, and a very hard worker. Those are the reasons I've allowed him to trap on our land all these years—why I allowed him as a companion for your out-of-school hours when you were young and had no siblings to keep you company. It's why I continue to hire him for the odd jobs I need completed around the house. But I will stop hiring him if you do not learn to keep your distance."

"But—"

"No. It isn't proper and you're only giving the poor man false hope. I will never concede to your lowering yourself to such a level, when you might have a well-connected, successful man of fortune, who can provide for you the life that you deserve. A man who can take you away from Millsworth and afford you the types of opportunities we do not have here. Why do you think I sent you to visit your aunt for so long? Do you think I enjoyed having you gone? But your mother says you would not encourage any of the men who showed interest in you. That you insisted upon returning home."

None of those men had truly been interested in *her*. Their only interest was in the family and business connections her father maintained in their grand, old city. Not one of them would bother fetching water for her. They'd order a servant to perform the task, then take all the credit of assisting her. "Those men were snobbish bores, Father. If you'd been there—"

"If I'd been there, you'd be engaged by now. I would not have coddled you as your mother did. But I was stuck here, still working to undo the mess the previous manager left behind."

A mess he'd stated would take less than a year to rectify, but which had proved more complicated when it was discovered the unscrupulous man had not only absconded with half the bank's money, but burned every last record as well. When Mother discovered Father would be required to stay in Millsworth for an indefinite period of time, she boarded the first ship headed for the tiny river town—leaving the servants to pack their things, including Nora, and deliver them one month later. Despite Mother's continual nagging to return east, a succession of potential replacement managers failed to meet Father's standards and their time in Millsworth had continued.

Father leaned forward, the leather creaking beneath him. "But don't you worry."

Nora's gut sank at the spark in his eye.

"I've nearly finished training Stanley and he's proving just the sort of man I knew he would be." He pointed at her. "Give me six more months to see him firmly settled and we'll be back in Boston. Mark my words." He nodded. "So if you're *determined* to choose a husband from this wretched excuse of a town, you'd better set your sites on Henry Davidson. That young man is the *only* man in this town with an ounce of true potential. In fact, I've already arranged several interviews for him through my connections in Boston. He'll be coming with us when we leave."

"But I hate Boston." Boston was crowded, noisy, and full of people who looked down on her for the slightest fashion faux pas. A life there would equal that of a caged bird. She'd be safe and well fed, but trapped into behaving as others expected of her, never free to fly. Millsworth may be small and settled, but at least it was peaceful and she was free to be herself among the people here. Especially with Jim. He may not see her as a woman, yet, but he'd never tried to change her or order her back inside *where girls belonged.* "Can't I remain in Millsworth?"

"You don't hate Boston. You don't know it well enough to hate it." He smacked the top of his desk, causing the papers to flutter. "I *told* your mother it was a bad idea, raising you here these last twelve years. You've grown too wild. Too accustomed to how things are done in the country." He straightened, holding her gaze. "But don't you worry. Next time you go, I'll be with you. It'll be different and you'll learn to love it."

"But—"

"You may go." Father waved a dismissive hand as his gaze returned to his ledger.

Nora's shoulders sagged. Once Father set his mind to something, he rarely changed it—and not once had she been successful in the attempt. She turned toward the door.

"Remember what I said about Brooks. You'll only be hurting him."

Nora straightened. A man who didn't care couldn't be hurt, and if Jim Brooks ever cared for her, she'd never hurt him. No matter what Father said.

"Would you look at this!" Nora stormed into the front parlor. "It's ruined!"

Jim's hand jerked, sending a smear of dark red paint off the side of the woodwork.

Nora cringed as he hastened to wipe the paint from the wall. After leaving her father's study, she'd retreated to her room to formulate a plan. She had six months. Only six months to convince Jim Brooks that she was the wife for him. To do that, she needed to change his view of her as a young girl and show him the grown woman she'd become. But that required time in his presence. So the first step in her plan was to secure that time. Unfortunately, she'd neglected to consider that her dramatic entrance might startle him

Jim pulled his hand from the wall. No damage remained.

She suppressed a sigh of relief and shook the wide, cream-colored ribbon in his face. "Just look at this lovely ribbon. Absolutely ruined by that paint you dropped on me!" He didn't need to know that that particular ribbon was at least three years old and her least favorite accessory. She needed him to feel bad about the blue specks it now sported if her plan was to succeed.

Jim considered the ribbon, then lifted his somber gaze. "I'm very sorry. I'll replace it, of course."

She nearly grinned, but caught herself in time. "Of course you will. It was your fault, after all." Thankfully, he was too much of a gentleman to point out that she'd dismissed the paint dripping as a blameless accident earlier. "I'll expect you here first thing tomorrow morning. Don't be late." Nora pivoted and strode toward the door.

"Be late for what?" Jim called after her.

She didn't pause, didn't give him time to rescind his agreement. "You're taking me shopping for a new one, of course."

Jim shuffled through the front door of his family's home in a daze. How in the world had he gotten himself into such a mess? Ribbon shopping? With Nora Taylor? The town gossips' tongues would be wagging for weeks. He swallowed. What would Henry think?

As if Jim's thoughts had conjured him, Henry strode through the door with a wide grin on his face, his brown hair mussed by the ride from town. "Mr. Taylor is amazing!"

Ma chuckled as she entered the front room. "You say that every day."

Jim looked around the room—their only room aside from the three bedrooms Otto had tacked onto the back. They didn't have anything so fancy as a front parlor for greeting guests or a study for...whatever rich men used their studies for. In Jim's family, everything but sleeping and cooking happened right here in this simple room with its worn-out furniture and unpainted wood walls. His hand tightened around the handle of his wooden toolbox. Thanks to the special deal the grocer had given him for buying so much paint, he was going to surprise Ma with a beautiful coat of blue paint for her birthday—albeit a few days late. She'd love it just the same.

"Jim?" Ma's voice brought his gaze to hers. "What're you doing with that? You know what I feel about you boys leaving your tools around the house."

Henry crossed the room and kissed Ma's cheek, his glasses sliding low on his nose. He pushed them back. "Wait until I tell you what he's done, Ma!"

"Who?" Ma's gaze flicked back and forth between her two sons. "Jim?"

Jim grinned and kissed her cheek. "I know the rules, Ma, but I've a surprise for you."

"I'm going to Boston!" Henry declared.

Ma gaped at him. "You're what?"

Amanda burst through the kitchen door. "What'd you say?"

"I'm going to Boston!" He pushed his spectacles closer to the bridge of his nose. "Isn't that fantastic?"

Ma sank into her rocker. "But how? Why?"

"When're you leaving? Will you be gone long?" Amanda took a seat in her usual chair beside Ma.

Jim set his toolbox on the floor against the wall. His surprise would have to wait.

"Mr. Taylor's arranged several interviews for me." Henry's chest puffed out. "I'm going to be a banker. And not just a teller like I am now."

Ma blinked. "What're you talking 'bout?"

Amanda's nose crinkled. "What more is there?"

"Well, I'll start off as someone's assistant, but Mr. Taylor says that if I do well, I'll be a manager just like him someday."

Jim scoffed. "Mr. Taylor ain't no manager. He's been managing our bank here, sure. But that's only ever been temporary. He's got important connections back in Boston. Not to mention all the money he's got."

Henry scowled. "You think I don't know that? Mr. Taylor says once I'm a manager, there will be things I can do, investments I can make to better myself."

Ma placed a hand over her heart. "But have you got to go all the way to Boston?"

"Mr. Taylor says that's where the opportunities are. He's promised to help me in any way he can. I can't believe how generous he's being."

Jim lowered himself into his usual hide chair, prepared to wait out his little brother's excitement. Once Henry got going on the things

"Mr. Taylor said," it took him a while to lose steam again. You'd think the man was God with the way Henry memorized his every word. Granted, Mr. Taylor *had* been extra kind toward Henry. The wealthy banker made no secret of his disdain for their small town, but he had a reputation for hard work, ethical dealings, and a habit of rewarding those he viewed as having potential. And Mr. Taylor'd made it very clear over the past year that he believed Henry had potential. Jim supposed he couldn't blame Henry for being excited. If Mr. Taylor followed through on his promises to open doors—and it sounded like he planned to—Henry was smart enough and hard working enough to turn those opportunities into gold. Still, Jim found himself struggling to get excited about the idea of Henry living so far away.

Ma nodded. "He has been incredibly generous, spending so much time teaching you about his business." Tears shimmered in her eyes. "But Boston's awfully far away."

"It's not forever, Ma." Henry strode over and took Ma's hand. "I'll come back to visit when I can. And you know I'll send money home. Maybe even enough to buy Mr. Taylor's own property. He won't need it once he's back in Boston. Just imagine moving in to that fine home."

Ma blinked and the tears were gone with a sniff. "I don't need no fine home." She caressed the arm of her rocking chair. "Your pa's done right fine in providing for us."

Henry nodded. "You're right, but think of how many acres that house sits on. You know Pa'd be thrilled to get his hands on it."

Jim snorted. "Course he would. Mr. Taylor ain't even using the property. Just lets it grow wild and—"

"Which is exactly why the rabbits like living there so much." Henry scowled. "A fact you've benefited from for years. Remind me, how much did you earn last month selling those pelts?"

Jim opened his mouth to remind Henry that his pelts had paid for the nice suit he wore to the bank every day, but Amanda cut him off.

"But what about Nora?" She leaned toward Henry. "How'll you court her if you're all the way in Boston? I thought you were set on marrying her?"

Jim snapped his lips together with a grimace he hid by pretending to inspect a small hole in his sleeve and lifting an arm to hide his face.

"I do. Nora's coming with me."

Jim's arm fell. He gaped at his brother. "She agreed to marry you? When?"

Henry's face turned tomato-red and he adjusted his spectacles. "No. I mean, her whole family is coming. That is, *I'm* going with *them*. Mr. Taylor says he'll be finished here soon and when they move back to Boston, he's taking me with him."

Ma pulled her knitting from the basket beside her chair. "That's good. He wouldn't have offered to do that if he wanted to keep you away from Nora." She started her rocker moving as her needles began clacking. "I was a might worried when you first said you was going to marry her. Wasn't sure how her Pa would take to the idea, but if he's offered to take you with them..." She let her words hang a moment as she stared off toward the front door before nodding again. "He must be thinking on the idea."

"That's what I thought." Henry fairly bounced on his feet. "That's why I'm planning to go see her. See what she thinks of the idea."

"How could she not be pleased to have a nice young man like you wanting to court her?" Ma sniffed. "That young lady doesn't put on airs like her mama. She's a right sensible girl. Kind, too. I can't see her turning you down." Ma's eyes drifted toward Jim. "Unless she's already set her heart on another."

Why was Ma looking at him? The moment by the well shoved its way into Jim's mind. He shoved it back. Pure nonsense. Jim resumed his sleeve inspection. He'd have to patch it. No matter his earlier foolishness, Nora Taylor wouldn't take notice of a man like him. He couldn't even spare the cost of fabric for a new shirt, never mind one of those fancy buttons on the dress she'd been wearing earlier.

Ma lifted her nose and sniffed the air. "Amanda, I think you'd better check those biscuits."

"Oh!" Amanda jumped to her feet and disappeared into the kitchen.

From the corner of his eye, he saw Ma turn back to Henry. "Did you ask her father for permission to call?"

"Well, I thought about it, but then I thought, what would be the point if she wasn't amenable to the notion?"

Ma paused her rocker. "Haven't you any idea of the girl's feelings?"

"Well, I haven't had much chance to talk with her." Henry sank into his own seat, his excitement seeming to leave him at last. "You know how strict her ma is about who she talks with and where she goes. I don't think she's left her house but twice since she got home from Boston."

Jim could feel Ma's eyes on him.

"Jim, what do you think of all this? You've spent a good amount of time at the Taylors' house. Does Nora have romantic notions about anyone that you know of?"

Again, the scene by the well flashed through Jim's mind. For the briefest of moments it had looked like Nora was leaning toward him—lifting onto her toes, even. But that couldn't be true. He must have imagined it. Why would a smart, beautiful, wealthy woman like Nora Taylor have the slightest bit of interest in a dumb, poor farmer with absolutely no potential at all? The notion was crazy as tying bows on a sow. He grinned, remembering the day he'd found eleven-year-old Nora in her father's pen trying to tie a bow around the neck of their sow. She insisted her father wouldn't kill the pig for supper if she could make him see how pretty it was. Jim had told her she was crazy.

"Jim?" Ma's voice intruded on the memory. "Weren't you listening? Do you know if Nora's set her cap at anyone?"

Jim scowled. "What makes you think I've got any idea what's going on in that woman's head?"

His mother stopped rocking and blinked, her brows raising.

"Sorry, Ma." Jim ran a hand down his face. "I guess I'm more tired than I thought. I shouldn't be taking it out on you. My apologies."

She reached across to pat his hand. "That's all right, dear. Apology accepted." She returned to rocking and looked to Henry. "When do you plan on going to see her?"

"Well, I don't know what time a lady such as her might rise, so I was thinking sometime later in the morning, to be sure she's comfortable receiving callers."

"She won't be there." Jim jumped to his feet, suddenly restless. He paced to the window. What had he been thinking, agreeing to take Nora Taylor shopping for ribbons? Paint accident or no, the idea made as much sense as a bow on a—Jim cut the thought short. He needed to come up with a new way of thinking about crazy.

"What do you mean, 'she won't be there'?" Henry's brows knit together.

"You know what?" Jim stomped across the room and snatched up his toolbox. He'd tell Ma about the surprise later. "There were an accident with the paint today and I told Nor—er, Miss Taylor that I'd take her shopping to make things right, but I got a lot of work around here that needs seeing to. Why don't you go in my place?"

Henry's face lit up. "You mean it?"

Did he? It was one thing not getting in his little brother's way; it was another serving the woman up on a silver platter.

"Does her father know about this arrangement?" Ma sounded skeptical.

Come to think of it, Jim also doubted Mr. Taylor would approve of Jim escorting his daughter in public. Though Mr. Taylor was kind enough to offer Jim employment now and then, he'd never shown Jim the special attention he paid Henry. Jim had no doubt, in the eyes of

Mr. Taylor—and just about everyone else in this town—Henry was a step above the rest of them, destined for greatness.

Nora deserved greatness. But could he really hand over what might be his last chance to spend time with her?

He looked at Henry's excited, puppy-dog expression. Oh, what difference did it make? Nora Taylor weren't never going to marry Jim anyhow. The idea was crazy as—his teeth clenched. He had to stop thinking that way. Striding across the room, he tossed his answer over his shoulder as he flung the front door wide. "Yes. I'm sure."

Chapter 4

Henry pulled the wagon to a stop on the Taylor's cobblestoned front drive and leapt to the ground. Pausing, he listened. Silence greeted him. Was he too early? Or too late?

Jim had instructed Henry to be at the Taylors' house "first thing" but refused to be more specific, instead saying, "You're the smart one. Figure it out," as he stomped away to work the fields with Pa.

He could be such a grump in the morning.

Henry shook his shoulders, freeing himself of his brother's negative emotions.

The sun had been fully risen for about an hour now. Would Nora be ready?

Only one way to find out. He leapt up the three steps to the Taylors' front porch, crossed the veranda, and raised his hand to knock.

Before his knuckles met wood, the door swung inward, revealing a scowling Nora.

"What are you doing here?"

Henry adjusted his glasses. Not exactly the greeting he'd been hoping for. And what was she doing opening the door? On the few times he'd been invited to visit the Taylor home, a servant had always answered his knock.

He yanked the hat from his head, clutching the brim as he bowed. "Good morning, Miss Taylor. I must say you are looking especially lovely today."

Something tapped against the painted wood flooring. Her foot?

She peered past him. "Where's Jim?"

"He, uh, he couldn't make it." Henry cleared his throat. Wasn't she the least bit happy to see him? "He had work to do back home."

"Oh." Nora's lower lip trembled.

Was she going to cry? Panic seized him. He never had any idea what to say when his big sister cried. The only thing that had ever seemed to help Amanda in those times was hugging her. He couldn't very well hug Nora. He'd better explain before she worked herself up to releasing the shimmer he noted in her beautiful brown eyes. "Don't worry. Jim explained what happened and I am more than happy to help you secure a new ribbon. In fact, I think you should choose two new ribbons. At my expense, of course." The cost of the ribbons would eat into the savings he'd been growing since he started work at the bank, but he could afford it. With his current salary, replacing the funds would only take—

"You've always been so kind, Henry." Nora smiled at him.

All thought of finances flew from his mind and he offered his arm. "Shall we go?" He couldn't believe he would be escorting beautiful Nora Taylor to town today. He resisted the urge to pinch himself. He'd set his mind to courting Nora the moment she'd returned to town, all grown up and shining like a rare jewel. He'd just never expected it would begin so soon. It had taken him months to convince Mr. Taylor to give him a position at the bank. Henry had expected it would take at least as long to gain permission to court the man's daughter. True, they weren't officially courting—Henry was still working up the nerve to ask her father—but this was close enough. For now. Perhaps he'd find the nerve while they were in town. They could stop by the bank and—

"I'll only be a moment while I collect my things. Would you like to wait inside?" Nora stepped to the side and motioned for Henry to enter. "Mother's in the parlor."

Nora led Henry to the front parlor where she left him with Mother before hurrying up the stairs to collect her outerwear.

Mary waited in Nora's dressing room, already holding Nora's green silk mantle.

"No, not that one. I'll stand out like a sore thumb in that, and poor Henry's coat would look positively drab beside it." Nora waited as Mary fetched a more practical mantle. "Did you see?"

Mary held up Nora's brown wool mantle. "This one?"

"Yes, that's perfect. Thank you." Nora turned so Mary could drape the garment across her shoulders. When it was on, Nora turned and Mary tied the bow. "He sent Henry. Henry! Of all the underhanded tricks..."

"Henry Davidson, miss?" Mary settled the simple matching bonnet on Nora's head.

"Yes. Henry Davidson." Nora tied the bonnet ribbon herself. Mary always tied it too snug.

Mary's brow furrowed as she passed Nora the white kid gloves embroidered with red and yellow flowers and tiny green leaves. "But I thought you and Mr. Davidson were friends? Wasn't he a monitor like you when the two of you were in school?"

"He was, though we never really spoke about anything interesting. All he ever wanted to talk about were the subjects we were studying and whether I thought a particular student needed extra help with an assignment. I wouldn't call that friendship, Mary. Friendly acquaintances, perhaps." Nora jerked her gloves on. "But that is beside the point. I specifically requested *Jim* to escort me to town. Not his dull brother."

"Then why are you going, miss?" Mary nibbled her lip. "If you don't mind my saying so, going to town with Mr. Davidson may give the young man the wrong impression."

Nora laughed. "Don't be silly. Henry Davidson isn't here to court me. He's here to fulfill his brother's obligation to right a wrong. Nothing more."

"If you say so, miss. But what of the people in town? Won't they get certain ideas seeing you strolling about town with an unmarried man? What if your father sees you?"

"We aren't going strolling, Mary. We are simply going to—" But before she could finish her sentence, the untruth of it struck her. One of the reasons she'd asked Jim to escort her today was that she hoped the townspeople would gossip about them. If Jim heard them being talked about as a couple, it might open his eyes to the fact that everyone else in the world had noticed she'd grown up. Had Henry noticed? Oh dear. The last thing she wanted to do was mislead him. He may be dull, but he'd always been kind. What had she been thinking to agree to allow him to buy two ribbons for her?

She'd been thinking it would make Jim jealous.

She covered her face with her hands. What a foolish notion! Jim wouldn't be jealous over someone he clearly did not desire strolling about with the brother he'd sent in his stead. She felt ill. "Mary, will you please go down and tell Mr. Davidson that I am feeling suddenly unwell and cannot go out after all?"

"Yes, miss." Mary bobbed a curtsy and turned to go.

Guilt pinched Nora's sour stomach. "No, wait."

Mary turned in the doorway.

"I'll tell him."

Henry cleared his throat in the strained silence of the front parlor, his gaze fixed on the clock resting on the unfinished mantel. He'd been unable to assemble more than one- or two-word responses to Mrs. Taylor's attempts to engage him in conversation. Evidently giving up the effort, she'd lapsed into silence four minutes ago.

Mrs. Taylor frowned. "Are you certain I cannot offer you some tea? Coffee, perhaps?"

The belt that had formed around Henry's stomach the moment he'd been left alone with the sophisticated woman tightened another notch. "No, ma'am. Thank you, kindly."

She took another sip of her tea. "Tell me, Mr. Davidson, do you—"

Nora stepped into the room, dressed to go out. At last.

"Miss Taylor." Henry jumped to his feet and offered his arm. "Shall we be off?"

Instead of smiling and taking his arm, she frowned and stepped back. "I'm afraid I'm suddenly feeling unwell. I'm very sorry for the inconvenience."

His shoulders slumped. "I am sorry to hear it." He examined her expression. She did appear pained, but whether it was from the distress of having inconvenienced him or from a physical source, he could not tell. "Should I fetch the doctor?"

"No, that is not necessary. It is only an upset stomach. I'm sure it will pass with time and rest. I'm only sorry to have wasted your time in coming here."

"The pleasure of seeing you, Miss Taylor, can never be considered a waste of time." Henry forced a reassuring smile to his lips. "Please do not trouble yourself on my account. I wish only for your health and happiness. The moment you are recovered, I'll return and we can secure those ribbons."

"Yes, thank you. You are so kind. Though, perhaps—" she glanced at her mother, then back to him "—perhaps when I am feeling well again, your brother will be free and you will not be burdened with the task of escorting me."

Is that what she believed? He must set her straight. "Escorting you could never be a burden. On the contrary, it is an immense honor, and I very much look forward to returning when you are well again."

"Yes...well..." Miss Taylor began to back from the room. "Nevertheless, I am sorry. Good day."

She could not leave. Not yet. He'd only seen her for a few moments and he'd been waiting all this time. "Wait!" She turned and he examined her again. She did not appear very ill. Perhaps rest was all that she required. The drive to the milliner's shop on the opposite end of town, though short, could be tiresome. Surely a simple conversation would not worsen her condition. "Could we not converse a moment?"

"Yes." Mrs. Taylor spoke up from her place on the settee. "That is an excellent idea." She waved to the space beside her. "Sit here, Nora."

"But—"

Henry offered his arm once more. "Please? I'll only stay a few moments, I promise."

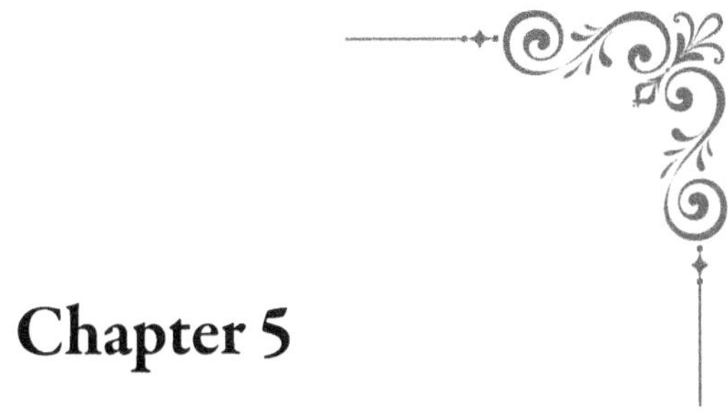

Chapter 5

Sitting beside Henry as their wagon jounced along the road, Nora ran over the morning's events again, attempting to make sense of them. Father had requested that Henry help haul the wood Father was donating to the Montgomerys' barn raising. That much she understood. What she couldn't wrap her mind around was how Henry had gotten the idea that such a request made him her escort for the event. When he'd arrived on their front step this morning and explained his intentions, she very nearly shut the door on him. Of all the nerve! He'd never even asked if she *wanted* him to escort her. Unfortunately, Father had heard the commotion and interceded on Henry's behalf, leaving her no choice but to play along. She was forced to ride the dusty roads on the open seat of Henry's wagon while Father and Mother followed behind in the enclosed carriage. The sad truth was she wouldn't have minded the dust so much if Jim sat beside her. As it was, she'd endured an endless parade of Henry's compliments for the full length of their three-hour drive. He seemed to believe her an angel sent from heaven who could do no wrong. How Jim would laugh at the notion.

Henry pulled the wagon to a stop amid the clamor and chaos of nearly every family in a hundred-mile radius gathering in the Montgomerys' yard. He jumped down and hurried around to assist her.

Placing her hands on his shoulders, she allowed him to take her waist and lower her to the ground as she scanned the crowd for Jim. *There.* Just before her feet touched the ground, she spotted Jim speaking with a group of men near what appeared to be the building site.

Stepping away from Henry's touch, she smiled up at him as he handed her the two pies she'd baked for the occasion. "Thank you. I'll go see if the women need any help." Before he could issue a protest, she scurried to where the women were gathering beside a line of rough tables made of several long planks set across tree stumps. "Good afternoon, ladies. As you see, I've brought my pie. How else can I help?"

Jim took a deep breath of the brisk autumn air, dropped the last tool into his box, and wiped the sweat from his brow. Finished at last, the new barn gleamed in the rays of the setting sun.

Ma held out a glass of cool tea. "Here you go."

"Thanks." He accepted the drink, and in one long pull he'd drained the glass. "I was thirsty."

"Apparently." Ma laughed. "Wait here. I'll fetch you some more."

She hurried off and Jim's eyes scanned the crowd as they'd been want to do all day. Searching for Nora. Again. He jerked his gaze to his boots, but not soon enough.

She stood beside Henry at the edge of the yard space chosen as today's dance floor.

His eyes lifted, but he forced his attention to where the musicians were still tuning their instruments. Several couples moved into the cleared area, visibly eager to begin dancing.

Was Nora eager to dance with Henry? The thought caused an ache that had nothing to do with the hard labor involved in raising the Montgomerys' barn today.

Having listened to Henry crowing for days about escorting Nora to this shindy, Jim almost hadn't come. Attending social events was never Jim's favorite activity, but the idea of watching Henry whirl Nora around on the dance floor made the event downright repulsive. If the

Montgomerys weren't such good friends, he'd not have come at all. But they were good friends and their barn burning to the ground last month had been more than a tragedy. With fifteen children and another one on the way, having a barn to protect their animals through the winter months was the difference between surviving to farm another year and having to call it quits, head back east.

Jim shifted to consider the fruits of the day's labor. The large log structure with its crude doors and simple rectangular shape may not be much to look at, but the angled roof would keep the snow from piling too high this winter and its thick walls would protect the horses, milk cow, chickens, and their feed through the long, cold months to come.

Ma returned. "Here you go." She handed him a fresh glass of tea, then hurried back to the refreshments table.

The music began, and like a magnet, his eyes sought Nora. She was weaving her way around the edge of the dance floor, darting looks in his direction.

He blinked. *Where's Henry?* Jim found him standing in the same spot he'd been moments before. Only now Henry's back was to the dance floor and Mr. Taylor was speaking with him. Did Henry have no idea his date had left him? Why was he not dancing with Nora beside the other couples?

Stopping a proper distance before him, Nora crossed her arms. "Well?"

He cocked his head. "Well, what?"

"I'm awaiting your explanation, Mr. Brooks."

"My explanation?" What was the woman talking about?

Her eyes rolled so hard they pulled her head along with them, making a full circle of it before returning to glare at him. "Do not pretend you don't know what I'm talking about."

"Who's pretending?"

"You promised to escort me to find a new ribbon, but failed to honor your commitment." Her lower lip stuck out. "I thought you were a man of your word."

Jim straightened. "I am."

"Then why did you reneg—"

"I—"

Mrs. Montgomery strolled up behind Nora, placing an arm around the younger woman's shoulders for a quick squeeze. "Nora, dear! Don't you look lovely today! And those pies you baked..." Mrs. Montgomery rubbed her swollen belly. "Don't tell anyone, but I've been back for thirds. I simply could not help myself. You must share your recipe with me!"

Nora beamed at the woman, all trace of the frustration of a moment ago vanishing in a blink. "Thank you for such a lovely compliment. But I'm afraid you'll have to convince Mother to share the recipe with you. It's an old family recipe and she's sworn me to secrecy."

"Well, I'll just see what I can do to persuade her, then." She gave Nora a wink, then settled her attention on Jim. "Mr. Brooks, I haven't had a chance to thank you for your assistance today. I saw you working hard—harder than some of the younger men, I'd say. I hope you've had a chance to enjoy our refreshments?" She nodded to the cup he still held.

He took another sip. "Yes, ma'am."

"And did you get a slice of Nora's pie?"

Jim swallowed, the memory of that perfect pumpkin pie slice still lingering on his tongue. He focused his gaze on Nora's shoulder. "The pumpkin was very good. Thank you."

Mrs. Montgomery shook her head. "Very good? It was amazing!" The first song finished, blessedly drawing Mrs. Montgomery's attention from him.

As a new dance was announced and the dancers took new places, he risked a glance at Nora.

Her narrowed gaze was waiting for him. A lifted brow let him know their conversation was not at the end he'd hoped it was. He sighed and shifted his feet.

It was the wrong thing to do as it drew Mrs. Montgomery's attention back to him.

"And why are the two of you not dancing?"

"I don't—"

"We haven't—"

Jim and Nora both spoke at once, but Mrs. Montgomery wasn't listening as she stole the cup from Jim's hand and set it on a nearby chair.

Taking both their hands, she joined them together and shoved them toward the dance floor. "Go! Dance! I insist you have a good time. You deserve it, both of you."

Jim hesitated and glanced about. Several other people were looking at him and Nora now. A few even waved them on toward the center of the floor with big smiles.

Mr. Redford waved his fiddle stick at them. "If'n you're going to dance, take your places. We're waiting on ya now."

Still, Jim didn't budge. He raised his eyebrows at Nora.

She shrugged. Her expression clearly saying, "It's not like we have a choice."

He nodded and led her to the center of the floor.

They took their place across from another couple, Jim still holding Nora's gloved hand. The music began and they stepped lightly toward the opposing couple, retreated to their starting point, and then released their grip on one another to change places with the other couple before turning round again. From there, the steps grew more complicated, involving at some point or other, several partner changes, forming a circle, hooking elbows, and moving in patterns somewhat resembling the number eight. Still, Jim didn't miss a step.

Thank you, Lord, for Ma's love of dancing. Though weary from working each day, Jim, unlike his otherwise agreeable stepfather, had never been able to resist Ma's request that he dance with her when the mood struck. And it often did. Which meant that while he did not have much in the way of book learning, Jim was the best dancer in the territory—or so his Ma claimed. Even so, he usually avoided stepping onto the floor publicly. Few of the local women had succeeded in cornering him into a dance, but each had complimented his dancing. So Jim was inclined to believe he *was* a skilled dancer, if not the best, as Ma claimed. Everyone knew mas were entitled to exaggeration when it came to their children.

At last, the song drew to an end and Jim made his bow before hurrying from the dance floor.

"Mr. Brooks!"

At Nora's call, he glanced back. No less than two men blocked her path to him, vying for her attention. Good. Holding her hand, even for so short a period, had caused feelings Jim didn't care to repeat. He hurried through the crowd and toward the Montgomerys' home. If he could just round the corner, he might find a moment of peace, out of sight from the crowd.

At the back of the house, he found a small wooden bench and sank onto it. *Why didn't I bring my horse?* He'd fully intended to, but at the last minute, Ma asked him to ride in the wagon with her and Pa, so that Jim could hold the two pies she was bringing. She insisted they would be safer in his hands than in the blanket-lined crate normally kept in the wagon for such things. As usual, his Ma's wishes had won.

Now he was stuck.

If he left now, he'd either have to walk, or leave Ma and Pa without a wagon to drive home. The first option sounded miserable. The second was out of the question.

So he sat.

And stared at the empty field.

And listened to the music and laughter as the sun sank below the horizon.

The crunch of dry autumn leaves being crushed warned him of someone's approach. Lurching to his feet, he scanned the area for a place to hide. That large bush might—

Nora rounded the corner.

Nora spotted Jim standing in front of a bench behind the Montgomerys' home. What was he doing back here? Had he been hiding from her this whole time? Coward. She stomped over to him. "I've been looking everywhere for you."

"I'm sorry."

Was he? He didn't look sorry. Instead of meeting her gaze, he kept glancing past her, as though searching for an escape. "You still haven't explained why you went back on your word."

Jim's gaze finally rested on her. "I did no such—"

"You did." He was going to deny it? It had taken every ounce of her courage to confront him earlier. Then he'd hidden back here, making her search high and low for him, when he *knew* they hadn't finished their discussion. And now he was going to heap insult onto injury by claiming he had done no wrong? "You went back on your word to escort me to town for a new ribbon."

"I didn't. I sent Henry."

"Henry isn't the one who splattered the paint. He isn't the one I asked to escort me."

He dropped his gaze to somewhere near her feet. "I'm sorry. I was needed at the farm. I assumed Henry would do."

Needed at the farm. Yes, indeed. As was any healthy male member of a farming family on any given day of the year. Yet Jim had found time to paint her family's parlor when her father asked. Jim had also found time to return and complete the job. Time when she'd been away from the house. Had he timed it that way deliberately? The question had haunted her for days. "Do you care so little for me?"

Jim's head jerked up. "What?"

"Is my presence that unpleasant to you?"

He stepped toward her, hand uplifted, but stopped just short of touching her. "Of course not!"

"Just be honest with me, Jim. I thought we were at least friends, but the way you've been acting..." She couldn't stop her lower lip from quivering. "It's like you can't stand to be around me." To her horror, tears welled in her eyes and she tucked her chin to hide them.

Jim's shoes stepped into her field of view, just at the edge of her dark orange skirts. "Nora."

"Just..." She blinked rapidly, willing the tears to cease. "Just be honest. I'll leave you alone, I promise. But I deserve your honesty, at least."

Jim's calloused fingers gently cupped her chin. "Nora."

More than the press of his hand, the gentle caress of his voice lifted her gaze to his.

He wiped a tear from her cheek with his thumb, his hand lingering on her jaw. "How could anything lovely as you be unpleasant?"

She sucked in a breath. He thought she was lovely? "Then why...?"

With a groan, Jim's hand dropped and he stepped back. "Henry's the one with the book-learning. The one with the future. The one your father approves of. And he cares about you—"

Pain sliced through her chest. "And you don't?"

Pain flashed in his eyes. "You know I didn't attend school."

He'd misunderstood her. She stepped closer. "But don't you care for me, Jim? Even a little?"

He jammed the fingers of both hands into his thick brown hair. "Of course I do! But that doesn't matter. I—"

He cared for her! Nora threw her arms around his neck and pressed her lips against his, visions of courtship, a wedding, and a small farm filled with little brown-haired, brown-eyed children filling her mind.

Henry found Ma talking with Mrs. Montgomery by the pies. She turned as he approached. "Hello, Henry. Where's Nora? I thought the two of you would be dancing by now."

"I thought so too, but I can't find her. I was hoping you knew where she was."

Ma's brows rose. "Why, no. But I've been so busy catching up, I haven't really been paying attention." She turned to scan the area and Henry followed suit.

Several couples spun and stomped across the dance floor while those without partners and those too old or tired to join in watched from the sidelines. Nora's stylish burnt-orange dress with its enormous gigot sleeves would stand out among the faded blues, browns, and yellows most of the women wore, but he couldn't spot her. He'd been searching for her since Mr. Taylor's attention had been snagged by Mr. Geoffrey. It seemed impossible Henry hadn't realized Nora was gone until that moment, and yet it was so. He cringed to think of how Mr. Taylor's discussion of a letter he'd received from his partners in Boston, though utterly fascinating to Henry's mind, must have bored poor Nora to tears.

He removed his glasses to wipe a smudge from the corner of a lens. What if she thought he'd only asked to escort her because of her father's business connections? He shoved his glasses back into place. He needed to show her he'd come for her—that he wasn't all business but knew how to have fun too. His eyes scanned the crowd. If only he could find her.

Ma patted his elbow and tipped her head to indicate a small cluster of older women sipping refreshments across the yard. "There's Mrs.

Taylor. Why don't you go and see if she knows where her daughter is, hmm?"

He kissed Ma's cheek. "I'll do that. Thank you."

Scurrying around the dance floor and the gathered onlookers, he approached the cluster of women facing the dance floor from behind. He was about to announce his arrival when the mention of his name gave him pause.

"I couldn't help noticing Henry arrived with your family this morning, Miriam. Has the boy finally worked up the nerve to ask Frederick's permission to court your charming daughter?"

Mrs. Taylor emitted a sharp laugh. "Goodness, no. Frederick merely requested his assistance with bringing the wood and somehow the boy got it in his head that he was Nora's escort."

Henry froze. What was she saying? Henry had very clearly requested Mr. Taylor's permission to court Nora. He'd spent hours rehearsing his speech and waited until Mr. Taylor was finished with his work for the day before approaching him. His employer was encouraging but cautious in his response to Henry. He explained that Nora had a fanciful side that could sometimes override her good sense, and that would need to be appeased if Henry's suit was to be successful. Rather than requesting to court her outright, Mr. Taylor advised Henry to begin by unofficially escorting Nora to this event. It would give her a chance to see him in a more jovial atmosphere than the somber environs of school and work she was used to seeing him in. His employer promised that once Nora saw Henry for the well-rounded person he was, Nora would not hesitate to accept Henry's court. Mr. Taylor'd even promised to assist in persuading her, should persuasion be necessary. Initially, the idea that Nora might need persuading to accept Henry's courtship had stung, but the longer he'd thought on it, the more Mr. Taylor's suggestions made sense. Which hadn't surprised him a whit. Mr. Taylor was the wisest man Henry knew.

Mrs. Taylor heaved a sigh. "When I realized the misunderstanding this morning, I thought to set him straight, but Frederick said to let the boy be." She huffed. "My husband has always had a soft spot for Henry. Sees a bit of himself in the boy, I think. Ambitious and smart."

Henry took a step back. Why hadn't Mr. Taylor informed his wife of Henry's request to court Nora?

One of the other women spoke up. "Henry's a fine catch, I daresay. He'll take good care of your girl."

"Yes. I'm sure you're right." Mrs. Taylor shifted her stance. "Though, I must admit, I still hold out hope she'll come to her senses and encourage one of the many fine gentlemen who came to call while we were in Boston. Not that Henry isn't a fine young man, but these men in Boston are from families whose connections could bring her to the very top of society. She would want for absolutely nothing as the wife of one of them. And their children!" Mrs. Taylor clasped a hand to her chest. "Oh, their children would have the world at their feet! You *do* understand."

"Of course." The other women all nodded sagely. "A mother only wants the best for her children."

"Exactly."

Henry stumbled backward, nearly tripping over his own two feet in his haste to escape before he was noticed. What a fool he'd been. Of course a woman as beautiful and special as Nora Taylor could do better than a nobody like him.

He whirled around, lifting his chin as he strode away from the crowd. He wouldn't be a nobody forever. Mr. Taylor had promised to help Henry rise in the banking industry once they arrived in Boston. Even now, interviews were promised him that would elevate his status beyond anything he could dream of in Millsworth. And he would make the most of those opportunities. He'd work every day—and every night—until he'd reached the very top of Boston's society. He'd become wealthier than Mr. Taylor himself, and shower Nora with jewels and trips to the continent. He was smart. His entire life, everyone had praised his intelligence. And he was a hard worker. Mrs. Taylor just didn't understand the gifts God had given him. Well, he'd show her. He'd show Nora, too. She'd never regret choosing him.

Stopping midstride, he scanned the yard again. He just needed to find her.

Chapter 6

For a moment, Jim stood frozen as Nora's soft lips pressed into his. *She's kissing me!*

A fire lit in his chest and his hands moved to her back, drawing her closer. His lips slid gently against hers, the taste of her far more incredible than he'd ever imagined. Not that he'd ever allowed himself to dwell on such thoughts. Now that he'd experienced such heaven, though, he wanted to go on kissing her for the rest of his life.

The crunch of dry leaves began as a dull itch in his ear, but as it grew louder, reality crashed in.

Someone's coming!

Jim jerked away from Nora, staggering several steps away. The backs of his knees slammed into the bench hard enough to force him to sit, just as Henry rounded the corner.

"There you are." Henry grinned at Nora before noticing Jim. His brow puckered as his grin faded. "Am I...am I interrupting something? Were you—"

Jim stood. "She was asking if I knew where you were." He bit his tongue to keep from retracting the lie. He never lied. The words left a sour taste in his mouth.

Henry's gaze shifted to Nora.

Thankfully, her blank face gave nothing away.

He looked back to Jim. "But what are *you* doing back here?"

"I needed to get away from the dancing and music." He rubbed his temple. "My head hurts." It was true enough. The moment he'd seen

Henry come around that corner, a throb had started in his skull like a hammer driving home a nail. *What had he been thinking, kissing the woman his little brother intended to marry?* No matter that she started it. He should have ended it. Instead, he'd drawn her closer—began picturing her as his own wife.

He couldn't hold Henry's gaze and studied the ground instead.

Nora's skirt shifted as she turned toward Henry. "What is it you needed, Henry?"

Thank goodness her voice was calm, even. Jim chanced a glance at her face. Still empty of emotion. Was that a good thing? Of course it was. Henry mustn't suspect. He couldn't ever know his big brother had betrayed him.

"I was wondering if you'd like to dance. With me, I mean."

The innocent excitement in Henry's voice threatened to drop Jim to his knees. He'd always been less educated than Henry, but he'd never felt himself a lesser man. Until now.

"Well, I—"

She was going to decline. Jim could hear it in her tone. She mustn't decline. It would crush Henry. "Of course she'll dance with you. She'd love to, wouldn't you, Miss Taylor?"

She stiffened, her shoulders going straight as a poker. Her nose lifted as her eyes narrowed at Jim, though her words for Henry came out sweet as could be. "Of course, I would. It would be my honor to dance with you Mr. Davidson."

Henry's gaze bounced nervously between them. "Are you sure? It seems like—"

Nora took Henry's hand, her smile almost convincing Jim of her sincerity. "Of course. You're the kindest man I know. It would be an honor to dance with you."

"Wonderful!" Henry fairly dragged her toward the corner of the house.

Just before she disappeared from sight, Nora glanced back at him, betrayal, confusion, and more than a hint of anger in her eyes.

It took every ounce of his self-control not to go after her, to explain that he hadn't meant to hurt her, that he would *never* intentionally hurt her because...he loved her. The dawn of realization stole the air from his lungs.

I love her.

He gaped at the spot he'd last seen her. He was in love with the woman his little brother intended to marry. What was he to do? All his life he'd been taught to protect his younger siblings and had gladly taken on the task. But now...how could he stand by and watch the woman he loved marry someone else?

He couldn't.

Jim stuffed his last shirt into the bag and took a final look around the room he'd shared with Henry since his baby brother was old enough to leave the crib.

Memories washed over Jim.

He'd never forget his mother's cries of agony the day Henry had been born. More than that, though, Jim would never forget the way she glowed when she introduced him to their newest family member. "This is your little brother, Henry. You're a big brother now. Do you know what that means?"

Jim shook his head, his almost-nine-year-old eyes fixed on the tiny, pink, wrinkled face peering at him from within the folds of a soft blanket.

"It means you have someone to look out for now. Being a big brother is a big responsibility. It will be up to you to protect him whenever your stepfather and I aren't around. You must do everything you can to help Otis and me raise Henry up to be strong, healthy, and happy." Ma held out her treasure and Jim carefully accepted Henry's swaddled form.

Jim tightened his arms around the precious bundle Ma had risked her life to bring into this world. He stared into Henry's little brown eyes and wondered what he'd be like when he was bigger. Maybe Jim could show him how to fix a broke plow or sharpen the kitchen knives for Ma. That way Jim would be free to help Otis in the fields more. Henry wriggled and Jim adjusted his grip. Henry's tiny arm broke free of the swaddling blanket. Jim frowned. With fingers that itty bitty it'd be a long time before Henry would be any help on the farm. Still, there was something about him... Jim traced his pointer finger over Henry's palm and all five of his tiny fingers curled around Jim's one finger. Something melted inside him.

Ma leaned forward. "Do you think you can do that? Can you help us look out for Henry, teach him right from wrong?"

Jim couldn't tear his eyes away from those tiny brown ones. "Yes."

"Do you promise?"

Jim's small shoulders straightened and he lifted his chin to meet Ma's gaze. "I promise."

The front door creaked open, jarring Jim from the memories. He ran a hand over his face as quick footsteps clicked across the wood floor in the front room, drawing nearer. *Ma.*

"There you are!" She burst into their room with a swish of skirts, her shawl still wrapped around her shoulders, bonnet still in place. "What on earth gave you the notion to walk all the way home? I couldn't believe it when Otis told me. I was certain he'd misunderstood until Mr. Montgomery assured me that he'd seen you walking away from their farm. He said you refused his offer to loan you a horse. Is that true?"

"Yes." Jim hefted his bag and stalked into the front room. He didn't mean to be curt with Ma but he'd intended to be gone before they returned. Goodbyes were a thing of torture and he'd hoped to avoid saying them today. Which was why he'd asked his stepfather not to inform his mother of Jim's departure until the party was over. Apparently that request had been ignored. "Where's Otis?"

"He's putting up the wagon and taking care of the horses." She waved a dismissive hand. "Don't change the subject. Why did you refuse Mr. Montgomery's offer? Why did you leave at all? I would worry that you were unwell, but I can't imagine you would have walked so far if that were so. Did something happen? You look upset."

Trust Ma to notice his unspoken emotions. "Yes. No." He let the bag drop to the floor, resigned to the tears he knew his news would cause. His chest already ached in anticipation. He hated hurting Ma but he couldn't stay here. He couldn't. "I have to leave."

"Leave?" She seemed to notice his bag for the first time. Her voice rose with every word. "What do you mean, 'leave'? Where are you going? What's happened? You can't just leave. It's dark out. We need you—"

"I have to!" He cringed. He'd never shouted at Ma. He yanked the bag from the floor and stomped toward the door. "I can't stay here. It isn't right—"

"But why? What isn't right? Wait!" Ma trailed him out the front door into the yard where Otis was just exiting the barn, lantern in hand. "Jim, talk to me. I don't understand."

Otis strode across the yard, his face growing hard at the sound of Ma's distress. "What's going on?"

Jim kept walking as Ma answered.

"Jim says he's leaving. Do something!"

Otis caught up with Jim as he entered the barn. "That true, boy?"

Jim dropped his bag by the tack wall and pulled a bridle from its hook. "Yes. I heard tell there's a new ironworks in Cleveland needing workers. I aim to apply for a position."

Ma gasped. "But that kind of work is so dangerous. Why would you want to do that? I thought you liked farming."

Jim jerked a blanket from the shelf and crossed over to Shadow's stall.

Otis stepped aside to allow Jim to pass into the stall. "I heard about the foundry too, but why are you going? Your ma's right. All these years, you seemed pretty happy working with me here. Thought you'd be the one I passed this place on to when the time came. What's changed your mind?"

Jim tossed the blanket over the stall wall. "Nothing's changed. I'll be back." He stroked Shadow's muzzle before slipping the bit into his mouth and sliding on the bridle.

Ma stepped forward. "Then why go? I don't understand. Did something happen at the barn raising? I—"

"No!" Shadow startled at Jim's vehement tone, taking a step away. Jim stroked the horse's dark brown hair. "Shh. It's okay. I'm sorry." He glanced sheepishly at Ma as he slipped the blanket onto Shadow's back. "Sorry, Ma."

"There's no call to speak to your ma that way." Otis's voice was low out of respect for the large animal, but his expression brooked no argument.

"I know. I'm sorry. I just..." Jim retrieved his saddle and settled it on Shadow's back. "I need to go away for a little while."

Ma laid a hand on Jim's shoulder. "But why?"

Jim cinched the straps, checked that they weren't too tight. "It's just something I have to do." What else could he say? He couldn't tell them he'd kissed Nora. That every moment, every step of the walk home he'd wanted to turn around and do it again. And hated himself for the feeling. Henry had talked of nothing but Nora for days and Jim had betrayed his trust. He'd betrayed the promise he'd made Ma. What kind of man did that? Shame weighted him as he grabbed Shadow's reigns and led him out of the stall. He couldn't look at Ma. "Please. Just let me go."

"But..." Ma wrung her hands.

"No point in arguing." Otis retrieved Jim's bag from the floor. "We've raised him right. If he says it's something he's got to do, then I trust he's making the right decision." He offered the bag to Jim.

Jim accepted his belongings. "Thank you." He led Shadow from the barn, Ma still on his heels.

"But how long will you be gone?"

Jim tied his bag to the saddle, then forced himself to face Ma. "I'm not sure. Maybe till summer."

The tears he'd known would come trickled down her cheeks. "But you'll miss Henry! He's leaving in the spring. You know that."

Jim pulled her small frame in for a hug. "I'm sorry." It was all he could think as her shoulders shook. *I'm so sorry.*

Otis offered his hand and Jim shook it, but when he tried to let go, his stepfather held on. "You'll be back?"

Jim held his gaze. "You have my word."

Otis grunted and released Jim's hand. "Good enough."

Jim hauled himself onto Shadow's back.

"Wait!" Ma shouted and dashed into the house.

Jim looked to Otis who just shrugged.

Ma emerged a few minutes later with a cloth-wrapped bundle. "Something to eat while you travel." She started to lift it toward him, then pulled it back to her chest. "It isn't much. Just a bit of leftover bread and a hunk of cheese. If you would wait till morning, I could fix you a proper meal. Even bake you a pie. I know you love my pies and I just got all those apples from—"

"Elizabeth." Otis's tone was soft.

Ma looked at her husband, and when his stepfather tipped his head to indicate she should hand over the bundle, she complied.

Jim accepted the gift and tucked it into his bag. "Thanks." He nudged Shadow to start walking toward the road.

"You be safe now," Ma called after him.

He cleared his throat. "I will," he called back without turning to look at her. If she saw the tears wetting his cheeks, she'd never let him go.

November 13th, 1832
Millsworth

My Dear Friend,

Please forgive my presumption in writing to you. Your unannounced departure of our small town has shocked us all and I find myself unwilling to live with the questions you have left behind. Might I ask why you left us with such haste? Did some pressing matter call you away? Were not matters here sufficient to keep you? The rumor about town is that you have gone to Cleveland and do not intend to return. I have dismissed this as ignorant gossip, however. A gentleman as fine as you would not leave me so confused as I currently am. In one moment you gave me every reason to hope, and in the next, you dashed it all to pieces.

Since you have gone, the first snow has fallen and melted away. The second snowfall is now upon us. It drifts, even now, gently downward outside my window. When I pull my curtain back I have a perfect view of our well through the tiny white flakes. Beyond it I can see the pigs in their corral and the fields putting on their winter finery. Do you yet recall those many years we walked together in search of rabbits? Much has changed since those days. The once-sweet memories these sights evoke taste bittersweet in the light of your abrupt departure. Why have you gone? Do you intend to return? What are your thoughts toward me? Please write and grant me the answers I seek.

You are always in my prayers.

Ever Your Faithful Friend,

Miss Nora Taylor

Jim let the letter fall to the blanket beside him. When the postman had handed Jim the letter this afternoon, Jim assumed it would be from Ma, or perhaps Henry. Instead, Jim found *Mr. Jim Brooks, Cleveland,* written in the neat, flowing handwriting of a well-educated woman. He knew only one such woman who might write to him. He couldn't believe she'd actually done it. Did her father know? It took him the better part of the night to make his way through the well-written letter—the fancy script of Nora's fine hand making the already-difficult task that much trickier.

He ran his fingers lightly over her words, wishing it were her skin and not her paper that met his touch. Which was exactly why he could not return to Millsworth. Not now. Not until her family had gone for Boston and taken Henry with them. A part of him regretted not being able to spend these last months with his little brother. They'd been close when they were younger, spending hours at the river fishing and swimming together. It wasn't until Henry's incredible advancement at school gained him knowledge Jim didn't have that the two began to grow apart. After that, Henry was forever wanting to talk about things Jim knew nothing about and it was difficult for him to commiserate with Henry's complaints about sitting in a chair reading and writing all day when Jim's entire being ached from toiling in the sun from dawn until dusk to plant the next crop. Still, he loved his brother and would have liked to enjoy what time they had left together before Henry went off to the big city. Who knew if he'd ever return?

Jim imagined Henry coming back to visit Ma and Otis with Nora by his side. He tried to picture Nora as Henry's wife.

The idea turned his stomach.

Jim would need to make himself scarce during those visits.

His eyes drifted back to the page. He reread her final paragraph. Memories. That's what he had that Henry didn't. Memories that went beyond sitting beside each other in a classroom. They'd laughed and played and challenged each other. None of which Henry would have thought to try with Nora in the Millsworth schoolhouse. Well, perhaps Henry had challenged her, but it would have been different. It would have been book-type challenges. Somehow, Jim knew Nora preferred challenges that didn't involve a pen and paper. She was always moving, always wanting to try new things. She'd never been content to just read about life. She wanted to live it. The day they'd learned about levers and pulleys in school, she'd come home and rigged a trap to catch a rabbit using all the new ideas she'd gathered. Jim had never seen such an overcomplicated thing in his life. But it had worked, of course. Because Nora Taylor was as brilliant as she was beautiful.

Jim smoothed his hand over the paper. He'd never have thought of it if she hadn't stated it so plainly. Jim's sole advantage over Henry was that Jim had spent a large amount of unsupervised time in Nora Taylor's presence. He was familiar to her at a time when many things were changing for her. But that weren't any reason to marry a person. Any woman ought to marry the best sort of fellow she could manage to find. And Nora Taylor deserved the best of the best. With Henry's natural smarts, years of book learning, and Mr. Taylor's promise to see him successfully employed in Boston, Jim's little brother was the best Millsworth had to offer. Nora just needed a little time to see that. He prayed Henry was taking advantage of the opportunity to secure Nora's affections before the Taylors returned to Boston and his brother's competition increased. No matter what else those big city fellows might have over Henry, Jim knew Henry had heart. Henry would do right by Nora and see that she was treated like the queen she was.

Lord, let her see the gift Henry would be as her husband. And help me to forget her.

With a determined set to his jaw, Jim held Nora's letter to the candle's flame.

Chapter 7

September 3, 1833
Cleveland, Ohio

The door to the foundry owner's office flew open, banging against the wall as Jim's supervisor, Mr. Langsley, stormed through the hot foundry and out the front door.

Jim carefully closed the door on the roaring furnace and stepped back. A hand clapped him on the shoulder and he turned.

Ned grinned at him. "I think Iverson's finally done it."

Jim couldn't return his coworker's smile. In the ten months that Jim had been working here, Langsley had been a poor supervisor whose unreasonable demands had led to numerous accidents and injuries. He couldn't argue with Mr. Iverson's apparent decision to fire the man. But Eric Langsley was also a father, working to provide for his family.

Jim had met Mrs. Langsley once. A few weeks back, she'd brought her husband's forgotten dinner pail. Her smile was kind and she'd had three small ones trailing after her. How would the family survive the winter without the man's pay? There weren't many well-paying jobs in this small city and only one foundry. Would the man move his family east to the bigger cities?

Jim said a prayer for the family before returning his attention to the iron charge in the furnace. He opened the small door and peered inside, heat bathing his face. The top of the charge was melted. It was ready.

He carefully inserted his puddling rod and began stirring the melted iron.

Beside him, Ned prepared to feed the furnace more fuel through a separate door.

Jim's shirt clung like a second skin, sweat dripping down his face as he worked. Unable to spare a hand, he tipped his head to keep a salty drop from reaching his eye. Work at the foundry was unlike anything he'd done on the farm. It demanded his constant focus, especially when he was puddling. Any distraction at this stage could lead to loss of the iron, damage to the furnace, or even serious injury. Yet something about the process of turning ugly, useless rock into beautiful purified metal that went on to serve a vital purpose fascinated him. It reminded him of how Ma was always going on about God taking the broken and sinful people of the world, cleaning them up, and using them to change things for the better.

Jim squinted into the bright golden glow of molten metal, continuing to stir as Ned fed the furnace. Ma thought God had a purpose for everyone. Jim wasn't so sure. He couldn't imagine what use an almighty God might have for an uneducated farmer-turned-ironworker. Not when there were Noras and Henrys around to do His good work.

After several minutes, the iron was fully melted. Using long tongs, Jim removed the ball of molten iron—the bloom—from the furnace.

Detre hurried over. "Mr. Iverson wants to see you in his office."

Jim handed off the bloom to Ned who took it down the line for hammering. "Now?"

Detre's brows bobbed up and down. "Right now."

What in the world could Mr. Iverson have to discuss with Jim? The only other conversation he'd had with the foundry's owner took place after the mishandling of a hot bar injured one of Jim's coworkers. As the only witness, Jim was asked to report the circumstances. That had been nearly a month ago. Mr. Iverson couldn't want to talk about that again, could he?

Jim closed the furnace door and put his tongs away. "You know something I don't?"

"Maybe." Detre shrugged, clearly enjoying his secret. "Go see him."

A minute later, Jim stepped into the foundry owner's office. "You wanted to see me, sir?"

The balding man looked up from his desk. "I did. Go ahead and shut the door. Then take a seat so we can talk."

Jim did as asked.

"As you may have guessed, I've just fired Langsley. Which means I need someone to take his place and see to it this foundry moves forward with fewer of the accidents that have been slowing our production." Mr. Iverson leaned forward. "It's been brought to my attention that the other men here look up to you. They respect you and listen when you make suggestions—even suggestions they don't want to hear."

Jim fidgeted in his seat. It was true the men seemed to respect him. Jim wasn't sure why. But he didn't like the direction this conversation seemed to be going. There were at least four other men working the foundry that knew a bushel more about ironworks than Jim. He'd only been here a year, after all. "Sir, I don't think—"

"That's why I've decided to promote you to supervisor, effective immediately."

"But sir—"

"I know. I know." Mr. Iverson leaned back, his attention already returning to the papers on his desk as he waved a dismissive hand. "You're humbled and grateful. Yes, and I appreciate that, but as you can see, I have a great deal of work before me. Now get on out there and let the men know they're to report to you from now on."

Jim sighed. "Yes, sir." At least he could see that the men got the breaks they'd been promised but never received under Langsley. That would be something. He stood and strode to the door.

"And Jim."

Jim turned.

Mr. Iverson's eyes narrowed. "No more accidents, understand? I expect a fifteen-percent increase in production by month's end."

Increase production while decreasing accidents? The men already worked sixteen-hour days, six-and-a-half days a week. Didn't Mr. Iverson understand exhaustion led to accidents? Jim opened his mouth to protest.

"That will be all, Brooks." Mr. Iverson nodded toward the door, his expression warning Jim not to argue with his instructions.

Jim swallowed. "Yes, sir."

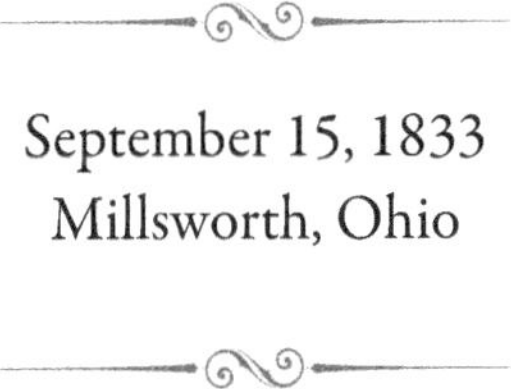

September 15, 1833
Millsworth, Ohio

Nora spotted Henry Davidson strolling up their drive and brought the porch swing to an abrupt halt. *Not again, Lord. Why won't he give up?*

As he climbed the steps to join her, she resisted the urge to bolt, instead pressing the toe of her shoe against the porch to return the swing to motion.

Henry had come to see her once a week, every week, for the past twelve months. And each time he asked her permission to court her. In the beginning, he'd only come on Sundays after church, at Father's invitation. When she'd developed a sudden headache each Sunday afternoon three weeks in a row, Henry began to vary the timing of his visits. Since then, she'd never known when he might arrive, only that he would.

He stood before her. "May I join you?"

"Can I stop you?" The unkind words slipped from her lips without thought.

Henry winced. "Of course. If you wish me to leave, I shall." He turned to go.

What kind of person was she to be so cruel to one who had only ever been kind to her. It was not his fault his brother had taken residence in her heart and left no room for any other. "Mr. Davidson, wait. I'm sorry." She waited for him to face her, then gestured for him to take the seat across from hers. "Please. Join me."

He hesitated, indecision warring clearly in his expression. "Are you certain? I do not wish to make a nuisance of myself."

Didn't he? Then what *was* his purpose in being so persistent? She'd made her disinterest in his courtship very plain over the past year. When he hadn't given up, she'd assumed he hoped to eventually wear her down. Perhaps he was succeeding at that, for she found herself smiling and nodding. "Yes, I'm certain. You can tell me about your day. Is there any news from town? Father hasn't returned from work yet and Mother has been in her room all day with another headache. I've had no other visitors and would appreciate a bit of conversation. I even tried speaking with Mary earlier but she was busy scrubbing the floors and shooed me away."

Henry chuckled as he sank into the chair she'd indicated. "I can't imagine anyone shooing away a woman as beautiful as you."

And just like that, she regretted inviting him to stay. Why must he constantly lavish such bombastic praise on her? It only served to remind her how different their feelings were for one another. But then he leaned back and began describing how a young boy sneaked a small snake into the bank that morning and the chaos that ensued when the boy suddenly shouted that it was missing from his pocket. Tears streamed from Nora's face as she clutched her stomach while Henry imitated the expressions of the horrified patrons.

A half hour later, the clop and rattle of the family carriage rolling over their cobblestone drive announced Father's return home. Bertram pulled the conveyance to a stop before them and Father emerged.

Henry stood to greet him. "Good evening, sir."

"Well, Henry." Father smiled as he approached. "Can't say as I'm surprised to see you again so soon." He raised a brow at Nora, though he addressed Henry. "How is my daughter treating you this evening?"

"Miss Taylor is nothing but kindness and charm, as usual, sir."

An undignified snort burst from Father's nose. "Yes, I'm sure. I've been meaning to ask you, any news from that brother of yours?"

Nora's breath caught. The question had been on the tip of her tongue since Henry's arrival, but she hadn't found a way to sneak it into the conversation. She'd never expected *Father* to raise the subject. What was he up to? She studied his face. There was something in the way he was looking at her. Confident, almost...arrogant. He knew something. Her fingers curled into fists as she shifted her attention to Henry who appeared as surprised by her father's interest as she.

Henry smiled. "Why, yes. Actually, I received a letter from Jim just this evening. It seems he's been promoted again—to head supervisor this time."

Her gaze whipped back to Father's. His expression hadn't changed. Nora's eyes narrowed. He'd known. How had he known?

Father turned from her inspection to face Henry. "Any word on when he might return?"

Henry shrugged. "He was supposed to return last summer, but then he got that first promotion and now with this...I'm not sure when he'll return."

Father glanced at Nora before facing Henry again. "Are you certain he still intends to return? He seems to like it there and he's obviously doing well. He'd be a fool to turn down the kind of money that position pays to return to the risky business of farming."

How did Father know Jim's salary? Suspicion snaked into Nora's mind. She knew Father had connections in Cleveland. Was it possible he'd had something to do with Jim's promotions?

Henry adjusted his glasses. "He'll return. He promised Ma and Pa he would. Jim never breaks a promise."

"Your brother is a good man. Still, plans change, as you know."

Henry nodded. "I know you had hoped to return to Boston months ago."

"Yes. Stanley's death was most unfortunate in more ways than one." Father shook his head. "But back to the subject. I must admit I had particular reason to ask about your brother."

Henry cocked his head. "Oh?"

"Yes." Father turned his smile on her and Nora's fingernails dug into her palms. It was his business smile. The one he wore when he'd backed his competitor into a position where they either had to concede to the deal he was offering or face financial failure. "I had a letter from a friend of mine up in Cleveland who hosted a dinner last week to which your brother was invited."

"Really?" Henry laughed. "I bet Jim was miserable the entire time." He sobered. "No offense, sir. I'm sure your friend hosted a fine dinner. It's just that Jim has always hated that sort of thing."

"Yes, well, perhaps he was not quite as miserable as you might otherwise guess. For my friend informs me that your brother has caught the eye of the foundry owner's daughter who is reputed to be a beauty." Father leaned forward as if sharing a great secret, though he didn't lower his voice. "They spent the entire evening conversing, to the scandalous exclusion of all others. My friend expects news of the pair's official courtship at any moment."

Nora forced her expression not to change. She didn't even blink. She couldn't. If she moved at all she might give away the crack that had just formed in her heart.

Henry rocked onto his toes. "That's wonderful news! Good for Jim! Whatever his reasons for leaving, he deserves to be happy."

Yes. Jim did deserve to be happy. Only he was supposed to be happy with her. Why hadn't he stayed, given her a chance to make him happy?

"I agree." Father clapped his hands together. "In any case, why don't you stay for supper? I believe Miriam has ordered a delicious lamb chop prepared for this evening. How does that sound?"

"That sounds fine. So long as Miss Taylor doesn't object to my joining you."

Her gaze drifted to Henry's beaming face, a question in his eyes. How could she turn him away? Why should she? Henry had never been anything but kind to her. He'd made it abundantly clear he cherished her, would fight for her. He clearly had Father's approval if not Mother's, and Mother would come around in time. Why shouldn't she give Henry the chance Jim had denied her? She forced her lips to curl upward. "Of course you should stay."

November 27th, 1833
Millsworth

My Dearest Brother,

What news I have to share! First, let me congratulate you on your recent promotion. Others may be surprised that you have been promoted so quickly, but I am not. You have always been an honest, dedicated, and skilled worker. It is only a mark in your employer's favor that he has recognized the value he has in you.

On that subject, a trusted source informs me there is another who has recognized your worth. They say the foundry owner's beautiful daughter has taken an interest in you and that you return her admiration. Is it true? I do hope so. You deserve such happiness as I have found.

Jim scowled. How had Henry heard about Miss Iverson's flirtations? At Mr. Iverson's insistence, Jim had attended the celebratory dinner party held in honor of the ironworks surpassing its productivity goals, with only one minor accident. The evening turned out even more arduous than he'd imagined. At first, Jim was flattered by Miss Iverson's wide smiles and extra attention. She was merely being kind to the new man in town, trying to make him feel welcome. Or so he'd thought. There'd been no way to misunderstand her, however, when he went in search of the necessary and she followed him outside. He still couldn't figure how she got the idea that he wanted to meet with her in secret. Nor was he certain whether he was more revolted by the idea that she thought him that sort of man, or by the fact that she was willing to compromise her reputation for someone she barely knew. Jim'd done all he could to discourage the young woman without embarrassing her. It took more fancy talking than Jim had done in his entire life, but she finally relented and returned inside, head hung low.

He'd waited several minutes before rejoining the rest of the group in the drawing room and settling into the farthest corner. He checked the clock on the mantel and counted the minutes until he might leave without causing offense. But for reasons he still did not understand, she'd settled herself such that she trapped him in his corner. He'd been forced to endure her flirtatious behavior for another hour before finding an excuse to leave.

He shuddered. Did Nora feel the same revulsion in the face of Henry's persistence?

Jim returned his attention to the page in his hands.

What a blessed time we are living in! You have your promotion and your new love, and at long last, I have Nora's acceptance of my courtship. You are, no doubt, surprised after these many long months, but it is true. Though I hardly dare to believe it myself. I did hope that, given enough time, I could convince her of my value as a husband. Though I admit to nearly losing hope on more than one occasion, the good Lord has seen fit to soften Nora's heart and reward my patience.

Jim let the letter fall to his lap. She'd agreed. After all these months refusing Henry's pursuit, she'd agreed to his courtship. Jim ought to be relieved. His plan had worked. Time had been all she'd needed to see Henry in a new light. Jim had worried last spring. The time for her family's departure drew near and she continued to refuse Henry. But then the man meant to replace Mr. Taylor at the Millsworth bank died in a tragic accident and the Taylors had been forced to delay their departure until the following January.

Jim frowned. It took her more than a year to accept Henry's courtship. Would one month be enough to convince her to accept his proposal? Surely Henry would propose before they departed. He wouldn't be foolish enough to risk her affections being stolen by some city dandy.

Would he?

Jim lifted the letter.

We have spent many a pleasant evening this past month conversing on her porch swing—under the watchful eye of her mother, of course. The more we speak, the more I adore her. I believe her affection for me is growing as well. I can see it in little changes to how she behaves around me. If all continues as well as it has been, I shall request her hand in marriage before this week is out. I have already received her father's permission to do so. I am telling you now, so that you might request permission from your employer to visit us and be witness at my wedding before we leave for Boston. It will, of course, be an unusually short engagement, but I am hopeful she will agree to it. It makes more sense to marry and establish our new home together right from the start than to move and then marry, which would necessitate moving yet again. I'm sure you'll…

Jim closed his eyes, unable to continue reading. He should be glad. Henry's plans to secure Nora as his wife before leaving for Boston were wise. It was what Jim had hoped for during the past year. It was the entire reason he had uprooted his life and come to this strange city to work in the hot, smelly ironworks. So why did he feel empty? Like someone had taken his stepfather's shovel and dug the heart from Jim's chest.

Chapter 8

Henry pushed back from the Taylors' table. "That cake was simply amazing, Mrs. Taylor." In truth, Henry hadn't tasted any of the food he forced himself to chew and swallow—but he was certain it had been delicious. The food in this house was always delicious. He was simply too overcome with nerves to appreciate anything this evening. He barely remembered a word he'd said over the course of supper and prayed he hadn't made a fool of himself.

Nora's mother smiled. "Thank you, I'll be sure to pass your compliment on to our cook."

Mr. Taylor assisted his wife from her seat, then grinned at Henry. "Shall we adjourn to my study and continue our game of chess?"

Henry swallowed, feeling heat rise in his cheeks. "Actually, sir, I was wondering if I might have a word with your daughter." He cleared his throat. "In private."

"Ah, yes. That's right." A twinkle entered the older man's eyes. "Yes, of course you may. Why don't you take Nora onto the porch? Miriam and I will find something to occupy ourselves in the parlor while you two settle things."

"Thank you, sir." Henry hurried to assist Nora from her seat before leading her to the porch.

They settled onto what he'd begun to think of as "their porch swing" and wondered for a moment if Mr. Taylor would agree to having it relocated to the front porch of the home Henry and Nora would share in Boston. He rather liked the idea of spending the rest of his days cuddled beside her on this swing, looking out at the stars above.

Nora set the swing in motion with a gentle push, but Henry drew them to a stop. The slight swaying set the food in his stomach to churning.

Nora shifted in her seat to face him. "Henry, I—"

"Wait. Let me speak first. Please." If he didn't force the words out now he might lose his courage and he was running out of time. "I know you only just agreed to my courtship less than two months ago, but when two people have known each other as long as we have and both their families are in agreement...and, well, with our departure to Boston happening so soon, well...I think folks would understand if we didn't do things in the usual way."

Furrows creased her forehead. "Henry—"

She was going to reject him. He could see it in her eyes, hear it in her voice. "Just hear me out, Nora. You know both my parents love you. I've spoken with your father and he's agreed to my request for your hand, so you know he approves. I know your mother hoped you would pick someone from Boston, but if you choose me, I promise I'll love you and cherish you for the rest of my days. And I'll work hard to give you a beautiful home and everything you'll need to hold your head high among the best of Boston's society. You won't ever have cause to be ashamed you married me. Your father has promised to help me establish myself in Boston and I won't let that opportunity go to waste. I aim to be the most successful banker the industry has ever seen. I can do it. I'm smart and I'm good with money, too. You know I am."

At last, a small smile tugged at her lips, though tears shimmered in her eyes. "You *were* the smartest one in our class."

"Except for you." Henry grinned at her, hoping to coax her smile wider. "You were the only one who ever scored higher than me."

"Only in composition. You bested me in all the other subjects." Her small smile vanished. "But Henry—"

"Don't answer now." He took her hands in his, squeezing gently. "Just think about it."

"I—"

"I'll do right by you, Nora. I'll make you happy. Just give me a chance." Henry leaned forward, daring to press a quick kiss to her pink lips. "Please. Pray about it. That's all I ask."

Nora blinked. Henry had kissed her. But...it was too brief, too sudden. She hadn't had time to consider how it felt. Gathering her courage, Nora leaned forward and pressed her lips against Henry's. She waited for butterflies to launch in her tummy, for her feet to float from the ground, for the world to vanish from thought as it had done when Jim kissed her.

But nothing happened. Though Henry wrapped his arms around her, no strange new sensations overcame her. No thrill of excitement or desire coursed through her. His kiss wasn't unpleasant. She didn't find herself wishing to pull away, but neither did she feel any desire to draw him closer. It was simply a pleasant experience. Kissing Henry was...nice. Was "nice" enough to carry a marriage?

She drew herself up, breaking their kiss. What a silly thought. Marriage wasn't based on physical desire or even romantic emotions, per se. Marriage was founded on commitment, common life goals, and most importantly, a shared faith in the Lord Jesus Christ. She knew herself capable of commitment, and Henry had certainly demonstrated his own commitment to their relationship. They'd had enough conversations following Sunday sermons for her to be assured of their shared faith. But did they hold common life goals? Henry seemed set on acquiring wealth, a fancy house, and a high social status. What's more, he seemed to believe they were things that would make her happy. After all the time they'd spent together, did he still not know her at all? Her mind skimmed through their many conversations and came to the realization she'd allowed Henry to do most of the talking.

Henry pressed another quick kiss to her lips, a dopey grin on his face. "Is that a yes?"

She dropped her gaze. She couldn't break this sweet man's heart. But how could she say yes to someone who didn't seem to know her at all? How could she say yes when her heart still longed for Jim? *Stop it. Jim is gone. He left you and he's found someone new. He's started a new life in Cleveland without you. So stop thinking about him.* She forced her gaze back to Henry's. *This intelligent, kind, god-fearing man loves you. He wants to cherish you the rest of your days. Why not let him?*

Nora sucked in a breath. *Just say it. Tell him yes.*

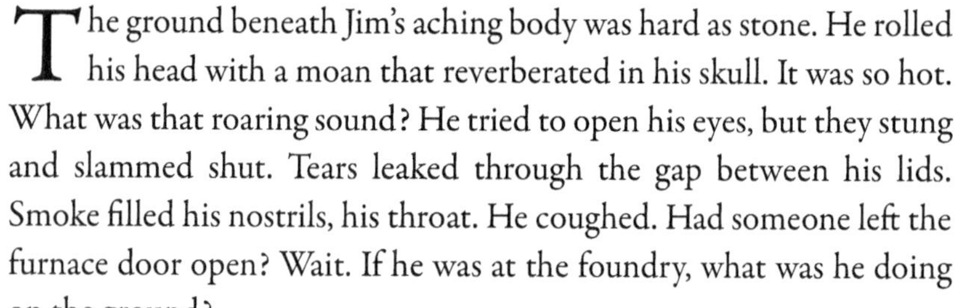

The ground beneath Jim's aching body was hard as stone. He rolled his head with a moan that reverberated in his skull. It was so hot. What was that roaring sound? He tried to open his eyes, but they stung and slammed shut. Tears leaked through the gap between his lids. Smoke filled his nostrils, his throat. He coughed. Had someone left the furnace door open? Wait. If he was at the foundry, what was he doing on the ground?

The explosion.

One minute he'd been extracting the bloom, the next...Jim vaguely remembered being thrown backward.

Where's Ned?

Forcing himself onto his stomach, Jim coughed and fought the urge to heave his breakfast onto the brick floor.

Jim crawled through the thick, black smoke, his fingers searching the ground before him. They bumped into something soft.

Ned.

He grabbed the man's shoulder and shook. "Ned!" Jim coughed and tried to speak again. His lungs wouldn't cooperate. Why didn't

Ned answer? Was he dead? Jim shook Ned harder, but his friend didn't respond.

Wrapping his fist around the man's collar, Jim tugged him away from the roaring remains of the furnace.

Lowering his face to the floor, Jim tried again to speak, to shout "Help!"

No answer came as he sputtered against the bricks, losing the battle with his stomach. Were the rest of the men dead? Or had they escaped the flames and smoke-filled room, leaving Jim and Ned behind?

Jim continued dragging his friend away from the spreading flames, his progress slowed by the weight of the unresponsive man.

Jim's stinging eyes narrowed to the skinniest slits—his vision too blurry to tell where they were. Where was the door? Surely they were close by now.

His eyelids slammed closed.

Please, Lord. Not like this.

Jim fought to pry his eyes back open, but they'd swollen shut. Coughs wracked his body. Shoving his hand along the floor in front of him, he checked that the way was clear, then hauled himself forward, still dragging Ned. Was Jim risking his own life to save a dead body? *Let him be alive, Lord.* Jim thrust his hand across the floor again. All clear. Over and over he repeated the steps: check that it was clear, haul himself and Ned forward another foot. Repeat.

Where's the door?

The air shifted. A wisp of fresh air teased his lips. He followed the direction it came from.

Moments later, the ground below him changed from hot brick to rough dirt. He kept crawling. Kept dragging Ned. The heat dissipated. The smoke began to clear.

He sucked in a breath of clean air and immediately began to retch.

Dropping Ned's collar, Jim waited for the heaving to stop. He swiped his hand across his eyes and tried again to open them. He managed to pry them a sliver apart. They were beyond the licking flames, beyond the walls of the foundry, lying in the dirt just outside the entrance.

Thank You.

His lids slammed closed and his cheek slapped the earth.

Chapter 9

Grinning, Henry leapt onto the Taylors' front porch and offered Nora the wrapped gift. "Surprise!"

Nora frowned. "What is it?"

"Open it and see."

"Henry, you shouldn't have brought me a gift. We aren't officially engaged."

"Yet." Henry winked at her, refusing to let her dim his enthusiasm with the reminder that she had yet to answer his proposal. The moment he'd seen these in the shop window, he'd known they were meant for Nora. They were beautiful, refined, and one-of-a-kind, just as she was. As soon as she saw them, she'd see how well he understood her. "Go on. Open it."

"I really don't think I should. It isn't proper unless we're engaged. I—"

"You aren't really going to refuse my gift, are you?" Henry affected his best puppy-dog look that always convinced Ma to let him sneak an early taste of whatever dessert she was cooking. "I've been waiting all day to give it to you. I just know you're going to love it."

"Well..." Nora nibbled her lip as she gave the swing a gentle push with her foot.

"Please?" Henry wasn't above begging to get what mattered most to him and he wanted Nora Taylor as his wife more than he'd wanted anything in his entire life. Anyone who held more tightly to his pride than the woman he loved was a fool.

"Oh, all right." Her smile bloomed as she pulled apart the simple string bow and pushed back the brown paper.

Nora's smile froze as she stared at Henry's gift. A pair of fine lace gloves. What on earth was she to do with these? She pictured the drawer in her room lined with no less than half a dozen similarly fragile sets. None of which had seen daylight since her return from Boston. Lace gloves had no place in the charming, but practical town of Millsworth. Gloves here were meant to serve a purpose—to protect one's hands from the elements and the rough surfaces encountered in day-to-day life in a small town. The gloves Henry had given her would snag and stain and do nothing to keep her hands warm in the winter. Nor could they protect her skin from the hot summer sun.

Henry leaned toward her. "Aren't they wonderful? The moment I saw them, I thought of you, because they're a perfect reflection of who you are."

This was how Henry saw her? Beautiful but...useless?

"Here, allow me." Henry snatched a glove from her grip and held it out for her to slip her fingers into.

This could not go on. Though she'd tried to share more of her heart with him in the week since his proposal, it was clear Henry still had no idea who she truly was. Nor did she believe he'd be pleased by what he would find if he stopped to really see her. Henry wanted a beautiful wife who'd be happy helping him achieve his dreams of financial and social success. Someone who thrived in the spotlight at dinner parties and enjoyed receiving such impractical yet beautiful fripperies. Not that he was looking for a superficial woman. She knew he valued her kindness and intelligence as well as her beauty, but he had no clue how different were their ideas of a happy life.

She pressed the glove back into Henry's hands. "I'm sorry, Henry. I cannot accept these."

"What do you mean? You haven't even tried them on. Go on. I'm sure they'll fit."

She nodded. "The gloves probably would fit my hands, but they don't fit my heart."

Henry's forehead wrinkled. "What are you talking about?"

"These gloves." She nodded to the lace in his grip. "They're beautiful and well intentioned, but they just aren't for me. Don't you see?"

Henry's expression fell. "You're talking about more than just the gloves, aren't you?"

She nodded, relieved that he seemed to be listening to her, at last. "You are a truly good man and there is a very blessed woman waiting for you to sweep her off her feet with your kindness, your integrity, and your promises of a prosperous future together. I'm just sorry she isn't me."

Henry sank into the chair across from her looking as though she'd just shot his dog. "But..."

She resisted the urge to draw him in for a hug. "I know you'll make some woman a wonderful husband some day, but you and I...we aren't a match."

Henry's back went rigid and his face took on an expression she'd not seen in him before. Sour. Like he'd smelled something putrid. "I never took you for a snob, Nora Taylor."

"What?" *How dare he!* Nora shot to her feet, the brown paper and string falling to the floor. "If that's what you think, Henry Davidson, then it's just more proof that you don't know me at all!" She whirled away and stomped to the front door. Twisting the nob, she yanked it open and slammed it behind her.

Rolling over in the dirt, Jim heaved what was left in his stomach onto the charred rubble that had been the front entrance to the foundry not one hour ago. Smoke still plumed from the gaping holes in its walls, incredible heat radiated from within. The bile coursing through his throat seared so painfully, it may as well have been the molten iron he'd been working day in and out for the past year. When his stomach ran out of bile, coughing shook his weakened body, dropping him to his elbows. His chest and throat tightened, threatening to cut off what little air he could suck in between coughs. He pressed himself onto his knees. He needed to move farther from the building. *Where's Ned?*

Jim turned his head, but fell forward before spotting his friend. Jim clutched at his neck. Air. He needed air. Why couldn't he breathe?

"They're over here!" A shout sounded somewhere nearby. Footsteps pounded closer. Someone tried to lift him and failed. "I need some help!" the voice shouted, then continued more quietly. "We'll get you out of here, Mr. Brooks. Don't you worry." Jim felt himself lifted by one pair of arms beneath his own, another beneath his torso, and still another lifted his legs.

"Ne—" Jim tried to tell whoever was grabbing his arms to help Ned too, but a violent spasm cut off Jim's words sending him into another coughing fit. His skull threatened to split in two with each hack.

"Yep. We've got Ned, too."

Good. That was good.

Chapter 10

The door to his room creaked open and Jim rolled over to see who had come in. "Ma!" The yelp launched him into a fit of coughing.

Ma rushed forward with Otis strolling in behind her. "We didn't mean to startle you. Here." She lifted the pitcher from the small table beside his bed and poured water into Jim's cup. She held it out to him, but his lungs wouldn't quit spasming long enough for him to accept it.

Otis stepped forward and helped Jim into a sitting position, easing the pressure on his chest.

The coughing slowed and Ma pressed the cup to his lips. "Just take a sip."

He did as directed and gave himself another few seconds to calm his breathing before attempting to speak again. "What are you doing here?" His voice sounded rough and wispy.

"Your employer sent a man to Millsworth to tell us about the accident and the fire and how you risked your own life to save someone else's. So of course Otis and I set off first thing to come and see you." Tears shimmered in her eyes as she took his hand and squeezed it. "I'm so proud of you and so glad you're safe."

Jim shrugged. "Couldn't just—" another round of coughing interrupted his words "—leave him there to die."

Ma tapped his shoulder. "Don't you go selling yourself short. You're a hero and nothing less."

"I'm not—"

Otis waved off Jim's protest. "Don't waste your breath arguing. You'll never convince her otherwise. Besides. I agree with her."

Jim scowled.

"Don't look at me like that. How many other men stayed behind to help you save that man?"

"None, but Mr. Iverson ordered them to get out." Over the past two days, Jim had endured an endless line of coworkers coming to apologize until he'd finally told Detre to just tell everyone no apology was needed. He couldn't fault them for obeying orders. Though, secretly, he wouldn't mind an apology from Mr. Iverson who'd run out with the rest of the men. Had his boss known he'd left wounded men behind? The explanation of events he'd learned from his coworkers hadn't been clear on that point.

Otis nodded. "Maybe so, but it was their choice to obey. They just as easily could have chosen to stay and help you rescue that man."

"But—"

"I said no arguing." Otis crossed his arms. "You don't give yourself enough credit. If you don't want to think of yourself as a hero, that's fine. But at least acknowledge that you did the right thing at great risk to yourself. You ought to be proud of what you accomplished. You saved a man's life."

Jim shifted against his pillow. He supposed his stepfather had a point. Knowing that he'd spared Ned a terrible death did feel good, even if he couldn't see himself as a hero.

Ma pressed the cup to his lips again and he accepted another sip of water. The lukewarm liquid felt wonderful gliding down his throat. "How long are you staying for?"

"Just for tonight. We'll leave at first light."

Jim frowned. "It's a long way to come just to turn around and head back again." Millsworth was a full day's ride from Cleveland. They must have left before dawn to make it here so soon after supper.

Otis nodded. "Yes, but your ma is eager to have you settled back in your room as soon as possible."

Jim opened his mouth to respond, but another round of coughing shook him for several minutes. By the time he'd regained control of his breathing, the fight had just about left him. "But my position—"

"We've already spoken with Mr. Iverson." Otis settled onto the foot of Jim's bed. "They're planning to rebuild the ironworks but it'll take weeks, possibly months, to get a new building up and replace all the equipment that was damaged or destroyed in the fire. No reason you can't spend that time recovering at home."

Home. The idea brought to mind Henry. And Nora. There'd be no avoiding them if he allowed Ma to take him home. "I can't—"

Ma poked his chest hard enough that Jim closed his mouth. "Don't you dare argue with me. I'm taking my boy home where I can tend to him and that's final. I won't hear any discussion about it. Do you understand?"

Jim let his heavy lids fall shut. "Yes, ma'am."

Nora stood frozen in the Davidsons' yard like one of those marble statues she'd seen in one of the fancy houses she'd visited in Boston. Her veins ran about as cold as that cool stone had felt, too.

She couldn't do this.

But neither could she make her feet move. Couldn't tear her gaze from the plain wood siding that hid Jim Brooks from her sight. He was in there, somewhere.

She'd been browsing the grocer's selection of soaps when the voices of two women drifted toward her from behind a tall shelf.

"I couldn't believe it when I heard."

"I could. Jim Brooks has always been the best sort of man. It doesn't surprise me in the least that he'd risk himself that way to save his fellow man."

"True, but did you hear about his injuries?"

"I did, and I heard the doc says he'll recover eventually. Jim just needs to rest, give his body a chance to heal."

Feminine laughter floated toward Nora as she pressed closer to the shelves.

"Have you ever seen that man relax?"

"I suppose not, but Elizabeth will see to that. You know her boys adore her."

"You're right, of course."

"Ladies, is there anything I can help you with this fine morning?" The grocer's voice put a stop to their conversation and returned Nora to her senses.

She hurried from the store and ordered Bertram to drive her to the Davidsons' home immediately. He refused to budge until Mother returned from the milliner's shop.

It had taken Nora ages to drag Mother from her shopping, but now that she stood before the Davidsons' home...

"What in heavens are you waiting for?" Mother brushed past Nora, striding toward the Davidsons' front entry. "After all that fuss about seeing whether those twattle-baskets in town were speaking the truth..." She huffed as she reached the unpainted oak door. "If you're just going to stand there staring all day, I suppose it's left to me to actually knock." And she did.

Nora hurried to join her mother, lest the door should open while Nora remained frozen in the yard like a frightened doe.

Seconds passed as they waited.

The Davidsons didn't have servants. Which of them would answer the door? What if it was Henry? She hadn't seen him since she'd rejected his proposal three days ago. When she'd convinced her mother to come here, she told herself Henry would be at the bank, but what if he'd taken time off to help care for his brother? Would Henry slam the door in their faces? He hadn't seemed angry when he left her house, but given more time to consider the matter, he might feel she'd led him on a merry chase and made a fool of him. That had never been her intention. But as she'd lain awake these past nights replaying the events of the past fourteen months in her mind, she imagined he might come to see it that way. She hoped not. She liked to think they might still be friends. He *was* still coming with their family to Boston in a month. At least, she hadn't heard of any change in those plans. Though, perhaps—

Nora's thoughts were cut off by the opening of the Davidsons' front door.

J im reached his bedroom door just as his sister swung open their front door.

Amanda smiled at their guests. "Mrs. Taylor, Miss Taylor. What a lovely surprise."

Jim lurched backward into his room, toppling onto his bed. A round of coughs shook him as he clung to the bedpost.

Nora was here. Had she seen him? She must have come to visit Henry.

The coughs eased enough that he could stand. Careful to remain out of sight, he took a step forward and reached for the doorknob. He swung it gently closed, wincing at its loud squeak. Dumb thing needed oil. He eased back onto his bed. He'd wait here until she was gone.

Reclining against the mound of blankets Ma had piled at the head of his bed, Jim stared at the ceiling. Even that brief glimpse shattered his efforts to convince himself her beauty was the trick of a faulty memory. *Why, Lord?* Jim had been so close to never seeing her again. If he'd remained in Cleveland just three more weeks, he wouldn't be suffering the agony he was now of having her so close, and yet so far. His eyes fell shut, the sound of female voices drifting through the thin walls—exquisite torture.

"I—I hope our coming isn't an imposition." Nora's voice wavered with uncertainty. Did she know he was here?

"Of course not," his sister assured her. "You're always welcome here. Please, come in."

Soft thumps on the wooden floor in the front room announced their acceptance of Amanda's invitation.

"That's so kind of you. Especially...well..." There was an odd pause.

Jim frowned. It wasn't like Nora to sound so uncertain. So timid.

Nora continued. "Is Henry at home?"

"No, he's still at the bank."

Jim's eyes flew open as he turned toward the bright light streaming through his window. That's right, it was the middle of the afternoon. All this extra sleeping had erased his sense of time, but surely Nora was aware of the time. Didn't she know Henry would be at the bank at this hour? His stomach tightened. What was she doing here?

"Good." To his surprise, Nora sounded relieved rather than disappointed. Must be the walls playing tricks on his hearing. "I mean, that is—"

Mrs. Taylor's voice joined the conversation. "Is your mother at home?"

"I'm afraid she's gone to visit a neighbor, though I expect she'll return any moment now. She hasn't left Jim's side for more than a few minutes at a time since they brought him home yesterday."

Nora cleared her throat. "How *is* Jim doing?" There was no surprise or confusion in her tone. Nora must have known he was here.

Before Amanda could answer, Mrs. Taylor spoke again. "We were in town today and learned of the fire at the foundry, though no details were shared other than that your older brother was injured and had been brought home. As good Christians, naturally we felt it our duty to see whether you might require any assistance with his care."

They'd come about him? It must have been Nora's suggestion. Mrs. Taylor never paid the slightest bit of attention to him, other than to relay instructions from her husband. For the briefest moment, pleasure flared in Jim's mind, but he stomped it out. He wouldn't see her. He couldn't. The pleasure of Nora's company would be too much to bear. Just listening to her voice made him yearn to spring from his bed, dash into their front room, and draw her into his arms. If he begged her forgiveness for staying away so long, for ignoring her sweet letter, would she forgive him? No. She wouldn't forgive him because he would never ask it of her. He'd done the right thing. It was Henry who deserved her, with his book smarts and bright future. Henry would provide for her as Jim could never hope to.

"Then you haven't heard how he was injured saving another man's life?" The pride in his sister's tone soothed some of his ache.

"No, please tell us."

Jim pulled a blanket from beneath his head and dropped it over his face, pressing the fabric against his ears. He would listen no more. The temptation—the torture—was too great.

Several minutes later a knock sounded on his door.

He ignored it. If Amanda thought he was sleeping, perhaps she'd leave him alone.

Another knock. A pause. Then the door creaked.

"Jim? You've visitors." Instead of Amanda's voice it was Ma's that penetrated the blanket. "Jim?"

Footsteps padded across the floor and his shield was tugged away. A frown marred Ma's lovely features. "Why did you have a blanket on your face?"

It was on the tip of his tongue to tell her he'd been trying to sleep and their conversation had kept him awake, but he'd stuffed the words down. He hadn't been trying to sleep and he wouldn't lie to Ma to save his pride. He settled for part of the truth. "I didn't want to eavesdrop."

Her look clearly labeled him daft, but rather than remark on his bizarre behavior, she eased him forward and returned the blanket to the mound supporting him. "I suppose that means you're aware Mrs.

Taylor and her daughter have come to see you. Shall I bring them in or do you feel up to moving to the front room?" She poured a glass of water and handed it to him as she'd been doing constantly since his return.

He dutifully emptied his cup before replying. "Neither. My head is hurting." It was the truth. The moment he'd spotted Nora framed in their front doorway the pounding in his head had returned. "Please tell them I'm not up to having visitors."

"I thought you said your headache had gone. Amanda said she heard you coughing a few minutes ago, too." Ma's eyes narrowed. "Jim Brooks, did you lie to me? I only went to see Bess because you promised me you were feeling better."

"I was. I am. I promise, I wouldn't lie to you, Ma." It was true. The coughing fit he'd had upon seeing Nora was the first he'd had since dawn. Granted he'd slept off and on throughout the day, but even now his lungs felt decidedly clearer than they had yesterday. His breathing was easier. "It's just a headache. I'm sure if I rest it'll go away again."

Ma studied him in silence a moment. "All right. I'll invite them to come back tomorrow, then." She turned to go.

Panic shot through him. "No!"

A gasp drew his attention to the door.

Ma had left it open.

Nora stood just beyond the doorway, her pain-filled eyes locked with his.

He shot off the blankets. "Nora! I..."

Before he could figure out what to say, Nora whirled away, disappearing from view.

Ma shot him a glare as he heard the front door open and close. "What has come over you?" Not waiting for his response, she hurried from the room, closing the bedroom door behind her.

Chapter 11

A few seconds later, Jim heard the front door open and close again. Mrs. Taylor must have left.

He closed his eyes and fell against the blankets.

When the Taylors had arrived, he'd been moving to the front room where he could listen to Ma and Amanda chattering as they always did while preparing supper. He still couldn't talk much without his throat catching fire, sending him into coughing fits. But he'd slept more hours than he could count since the fire, and lying in his bed staring at the ceiling had grown tiresome. Now, though...maybe he'd take another nap.

The door to his room clicked open.

He tugged one heavy lid up and spied Ma marching to his bedside. *Uh-oh.*

"Jim Brooks, you open those eyes and explain yourself. I have never been so embarrassed." Her hands landed on her hips. "What're you thinking, being so rude to a family that's been nothing but generous toward us for years? And don't you tell me it's because Miss Taylor's broken your brother's heart."

Jim startled. *She what?*

"I warned Henry he was headed for heartache when she held him at arm's length for so long, but he wouldn't listen. He was convinced he could make her love him if he just kept trying. It never did make sense to me." She poured another cup of water and thrust it at Jim.

He accepted and sipped the soothing liquid as Ma kept on.

"I knew right away with both your father and Otis that there was something special about them. No one had to persuade me to love them. But I know not all marriages start off that way and Henry's a grown man—" her eyes drifted to the window—"so I said my piece and let him make his own choices. And they were *his* choices." Ma's narrowed gaze snapped back to Jim. "No one can accuse that young woman of misleading him. She made her feelings plain from the start. So don't you go being rude to her on Henry's account."

"Ma." Jim set the cup aside and held his hands up. "I don't know what you're talking about. I thought Nora and Henry were engaged."

Ma blinked. "He didn't tell you?"

"Tell me what?"

Ma sank to the edge of Jim's bed with a heavy sigh. "Henry proposed but Nora never accepted."

"Never accepted?" Jim couldn't wrap his brain around it. How could she not accept Henry? Didn't she see how perfect they were for each other?

"Reading between the lines of what Henry told me, I think she tried to tell him no right away but he talked her into putting off the decision by telling her to pray about it. And praying about a decision is never wrong—especially something as serious as marriage—but in this case—" her shoulders sagged—"I think it just delayed the inevitable because a week later she turned him down and ended their courtship."

"She ended it? You mean...it's over?" Jim gaped at his mother.

Ma nodded. "The same day as the fire, actually."

This couldn't be. Nora was supposed to marry Henry. Henry was supposed to take care of her, provide her with the life Jim couldn't. But if Nora chose a husband in Boston, Jim would never know if she were being cared for the way she deserved. How could she do this?

Ma tipped her head to the side. "But if you didn't know about all that...what *were* you thinking? Why would you refuse to visit with the

Taylor women? It isn't like you to be so rude, and I thought you and Nora were friends."

"No. I mean, we are. We were. But—" No acceptable explanation came to mind—not one he dared share with Ma, at any rate. He started coughing.

A timid knock brought Nora's head off the pillow. She squinted through tear-filled eyes at her closed bedroom door. Hadn't she told Mary to leave her be? Yet it must be Mary on the other side. Father was still at the bank and Mother had retreated to her room as soon as they'd arrived home, another headache having besieged her.

Nora let her head flop back onto the pillow but tilted so that her mouth was free of its plush confines. "Go away."

"You've a visitor, miss." Mary's voice was muffled by the thick wood.

Nora rolled onto her back and swiped at her damp face. A visitor? Jim? Could he have changed his mind about seeing her? She was halfway to sitting before logic kicked in. Jim wouldn't have come to see her. Even if, by some miracle, he possessed such a desire, he was far too ill to come to her house.

She fell back again. She didn't want to see anyone else. "Tell them I'm indisposed."

There was a long pause before Mary's voice came again. "It's Mrs. Davidson, miss. I—I've shown her into the front parlor."

Nora bolted upright. Why would Jim and Henry's mother have come to see her? Nora nibbled her lip. What if she was angry with Nora for rejecting Henry's proposal? Had she come to tell Nora to stay away from their family? But no. That didn't make sense. She'd been kind and welcoming when Nora and Mother had stopped in this afternoon. It was Jim who'd turned them away. Jim who didn't want to see them. To see Nora.

Her chest squeezed and she thought she might never breathe again. After all these months, she'd hoped some of her feelings for Jim might have at least lessened. But the moment she'd heard he was injured, nothing had been more important than seeing for herself that he was recovering. After his abrupt departure and months of silence, she'd known there was no hope that he returned her romantic feelings. Their kiss at the barn raising had been a mistake. She'd thrown herself at him, and in a moment of weakness, he'd not stopped her. Shame still lingered with the memory. Still, she had hoped their friendship could survive the incident. Clearly, she'd been mistaken.

"Miss?" Mary's voice brought her back to the present.

"Come in, Mary." Nora slipped from bed to assess her appearance in the small mirror above her chest of drawers. Her eyes were red-rimmed, her cheeks shiny, and her once-beautiful bun resembled a bird's nest after the hour she'd just spent wallowing in self-pity. Nora found Mary's sympathetic gaze in the mirror. "Help me?"

Mary nodded and set to work. She dipped a cloth in water, wrung it out, and instructed Nora to hold it over her eyes while Mary corrected the disaster atop Nora's head. Nora did as told and allowed the familiarity of the stroking brush to soothe her battered emotions.

A few minutes later, Mary's soft voice broke the silence. "There you are."

Nora lowered the cloth to study her reflection once more. Thankfully, her eyelids were lined with pink instead of the garish red of moments before. The largest improvement, though, was the miracle Mary's skilled hands had performed. Gone were the ragged tangles jutting this way and that. In their place sat a perfectly coiffed knot at the top of her head. Her face was framed with the expensive faux curls Mother had purchased for her in Boston. Nora had never worn them before, preferring to curl her own hair, but there was no time for curling while a guest sat waiting. She eyed the curls closely. They were impressively deceptive in their ability to blend with her own hair. She sighed as she rose. Mother had been right to argue Nora would find them useful someday.

"Just a moment, miss."

Nora paused long enough for Mary to pat the dampness from Nora's face and add the barest dusting of powder. Then Nora squared her shoulders and left her room.

Mrs. Davidson sat on the settee in the front parlor. She rose as Nora entered.

"I'm so sorry to have kept you waiting. Please, do be seated."

Mrs. Davidson resumed her position on the settee as Nora took the chair opposite. "It's quite all right. I'm aware my visit is unexpected. Thank you for seeing me."

Though her heart still ached and her nerves rattled a bit, it was not difficult for Nora to find a smile for one of the kindest women she'd ever known. "You're always welcome here, of course."

"Thank you." The older woman paused, her eyes narrowing slightly as she seemed to study Nora. "My dear, please forgive my impertinence, but have you been crying?"

"I—" What should she say?

"Does it have anything to do with my eldest son's inexcusable behavior this afternoon?"

Nora bit her lip and turned her face from Mrs. Davidson's view. Pressing her lips tight, Nora blinked rapidly. Curse these wretched tears. She cleared her throat and took a deep breath. "Of course not." She forced her lips to curve upward and turned back to face her guest. "He is injured and miserable. Any man in such a state might be out of sorts. Jim—er, Mr. Brooks was clearly not himself. Taking his behavior personally would be silly. I—" Nora's gaze dipped to her lap. It was on the tip of her tongue to claim her tears had some other cause, but no excuse seemed suitable. And she did not wish to lie to Jim's mother. So she held her tongue.

"It wouldn't be silly at all, actually—" Mrs. Davidson leaned forward, lowering her soft voice "—if you're in love with him."

Nora gasped, her eyes shooting to the woman in front of her. "What?"

"Are you?"

"Am I what?" Nora's brain scrambled to keep up with the shocking turn of this conversation. How had Jim's mother ever suspected? Had Nora's behavior at their home this afternoon been so telling? Was that why Mother had scowled in silence the entire way home?

"Are you in love with Jim?"

"I—I—"

"Because I believe he is in love with you."

The chair might have disappeared from beneath Nora, for suddenly she was floating, upside-down and sideways, so radically had her world just shifted. "You...do?" Hope sparked in her chest, but something niggled at the back of her mind, preventing the flame from growing.

Mrs. Davidson's eyes twinkled. "I do. And I can see that you feel the same."

"But..." How could his mother be so certain? Something didn't feel right. "Did he tell you he loves me?"

Mrs. Davidson's smile tilted. "Not in so many words. But I know my boy." Her eyes lost a little of their twinkle. "I only wish I'd figured it out sooner. Tell me, what happened at the Montgomerys' barn raising?"

Nora's mouth opened and closed like a fish. Could the woman read minds? Had she been spying on them? Nora's cheeks flamed at the thought of what Jim's mother might have witnessed.

Mrs. Davidson chuckled. "I see." She nodded. "That explains a lot."

"But I haven't said a word."

"You don't have to. I think I've the way of things now. And it finally explains why Jim fled Millsworth last year. And why he hasn't been home to visit in all the time he's been working at the foundry. Why he looked so panicked by the thought of seeing you today."

The foundry. A memory clicked into place, smothering Nora's tiny spark of hope. "But he's courting someone else."

It was Mrs. Davidson's turn to look shocked. "What?"

"Father said that Jim was courting the foundry owner's daughter." The *beautiful* daughter, who was apparently as enamored with Jim as he was with her.

Mrs. Davidson shook her head. "I don't know where your father got his information, but he's mistaken. Jim has said nothing to me of courting anyone. And he wouldn't keep something like that from Otis and me."

Could she be right? Nora knew Jim and his mother were close. It didn't make sense that Jim would keep his courtship a secret. But Father had seemed so certain. He'd never approved of her friendship with Jim, but Father would never lie to her. She was convinced of it. So...one of them must be mistaken. But was it Father? Or Mrs. Davidson?

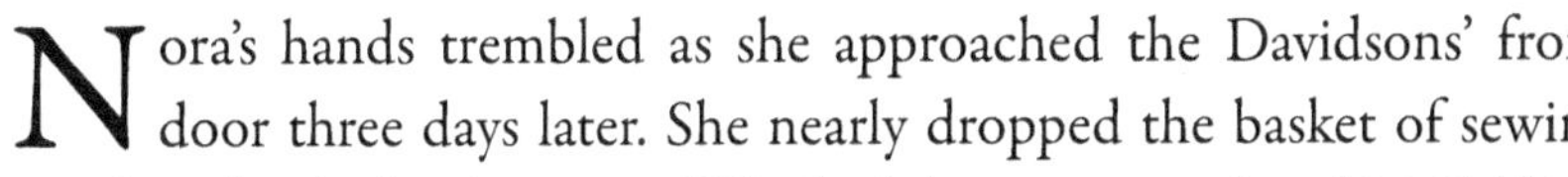

Nora's hands trembled as she approached the Davidsons' front door three days later. She nearly dropped the basket of sewing supplies clutched in her arms. Why had she ever agreed to this? Shifting the basket to one arm, she lifted her free hand and knocked. Lightly.

A heartbeat passed and no one answered. Nora whirled from the door. Oh well, she'd tried.

Before she could take a single step, the door behind her creaked open.

Nora froze.

"Miss Taylor! I'm so glad you could make it. Please, come in." Mrs. Davidson's cheerful tone betrayed nothing of the fact that she was speaking to Nora's cowardly backside.

Cringing, Nora pivoted. She plastered a smile on her face. "Thank you for inviting me."

Grinning, Mrs. Davidson waved a hand for her to enter. "Won't you come in?"

Nora's eyes narrowed. Was that mirth in the older woman's eyes? Straightening her shoulders and lifting her chin, Nora stepped past her hostess into the family's large front room.

Memories assailed her of the times she'd trailed Jim home after catching their rabbits. As a young girl, she'd spent hours following his mother around the house, learning things Nora's own mother didn't know how to do. The life of a farm wife had fascinated her. There was always something to do, someone who needed her. It was so very different from the hours her own mother spent writing letters to Boston, stitching endless piles of embroidered pillows or other fripperies, and ordering the servants about.

In light of her mother's almost daily headaches that kept her in bed for hours at a time, Nora often thought it providential that Mother had married a man wealthy enough to employ a full staff—including the series of governesses who'd raised Nora. The staff was able to keep things going without a hiccup whether Mother was abed or not. However, Nora had no such health concerns and often wondered, if she were to marry a man equally as wealthy, would her assistance be equally as unnecessary?

Movement in the corner drew Nora back to the present.

Jim stood from a chair near the fire, his eyes wide. "Good afternoon, Miss Taylor." He gave a stiff nod. "I think I'll just—" He took a step toward his bedroom door, but his mother's voice halted him.

"Jim Brooks, you sit right back down." Mrs. Davidson shut the front door and crossed the room to stand before her son, her stern expression brooking no argument. "When you begged me for something to do earlier, you gave me your word that if I let you out of your room, you'd stay put in that chair and not move an inch for the rest of the day."

"Yes, but—"

"Are you going to keep your word or aren't you?"

"Yes, Ma." Jim's gaze flicked to Nora's as he sank to his seat, his cheeks turning a slight shade of pink.

Nora pressed her lips together. This had been a poor idea. Jim was clearly no more eager to see her today than he was the first time she'd come. She turned pleading eyes on Mrs. Davidson. "Perhaps I should come back another time. Or I can just take the things you need mended home with me and—"

"Nonsense." Mrs. Davidson took Nora by the shoulders and steered her to the seat directly across from Jim. "You just sit right here and make yourself comfortable by the fire." The older woman hooked her fingers over the top edge of a small, open crate beside Jim's chair and dragged it to a spot halfway between Jim and Nora. "There you are. Now you can both reach the mend pile." Mrs. Davidson straightened and bustled toward the open kitchen door. "I do appreciate you offering to help with the task, Miss Taylor. There are a good many things I've let slip since Jim's been home. I haven't felt right about leaving him alone. But with you here to keep an eye on him, I feel safe turning my mind to those tasks. Thank you, kindly." She threw the last few words over her shoulder just before swinging the kitchen door nearly shut behind her.

Nora was grateful his mother left it open a half-dozen inches. It would still cause talk should the wrong person enter and find Nora and Jim alone in this room, but at least his matchmaking mother had preserved some sense of propriety.

Nora dared a glance at Jim and found him staring at her. She took a deep breath. "How are you feeling?"

He blinked and lowered his gaze to his lap. "Better than expected, actually." He reached for a needle and thread on the small table beside him. "I ought to be doing a whole lot more, but Ma insists on babying me, and Otis has banished me from the fields and barn until Ma says it's all right." He snatched a shirt from the crate between them and began working at its frayed hem. "Meanwhile, I'm stuck doing women's work." He scrunched his face in disgust, but there was an affection he couldn't hide in his tone.

Mrs. Davidson had raised both her boys to know their way around a kitchen, how to work a needle, and most of the other chores many men would consider beneath them. Nora had overheard the woman remind her sons many times that the skills would come in handy in the time between their leaving home and their taking a wife. She'd also confided to Nora that she hoped it would help her son's better respect their wives and the unending load of work most wives accomplished every day.

Nora pulled a skirt from the crate and searched it for wear as she spoke. "I'm glad you're not pushing yourself too hard. I'd hate to see you regress in your recovery."

"Re-what?"

She looked up to find Jim staring at her, his forehead bunched in confusion. "Regress. It means to return to a less developed state. In your case, to grow ill again rather than continuing to improve."

He grunted and returned his attention to sewing.

She'd irritated him.

With a sigh, Nora lapsed into silence and retrieved a needle and thread from the supplies she'd brought with her. Settling the worn hem of the skirt on her lap, she focused on sewing as well. Or tried to. How was she to concentrate on making perfect stitches with so much tension between them? Why did he frown whenever he saw her now? He used to smile when he saw her. It was one of the reasons she'd spent so much time trailing him through their fields. Father was always so busy with work and Mother was forever shushing Nora and reminding her to be a lady. Jim had only ever accepted her for who she was. Sure, he seemed mildly annoyed by her questions sometimes, but even she could admit she asked him an inordinate amount of questions. She couldn't help it. He knew so much that wasn't in her books. Things about life in the big city from before his mother married Otis and moved to Millsworth. Things about farming and fishing and family. His family was so different from hers. She pestered him with questions until he finally allowed her to follow him home and see their life for herself.

Through all of her pestering, though, Jim never once asked her to be someone she wasn't. He hadn't demanded she sit straighter, nor scowled at her for sharing her opinions, or sniffed in disdain when her skirts grew muddy from tromping along the riverbanks. As a result, there'd been a sense of ease between them—a friendship unlike any other she'd experienced.

Until she'd started feeling a zing on the rare occasions she touched him. Until her eyes started following him wherever he went. The ease had vanished entirely then. But that had only ever been on her part.

Or so she'd thought before that moment by the well.

And their kiss.

She still didn't understand Jim's part in that.

Yes, she'd been the one to throw her arms around him and press her lips to his, but he'd kissed her back. With passion.

And then he'd left. Ran, actually.

Why had he run? Could Mrs. Davidson be right? Had he run because of Henry's feelings for Nora? But what about *her* feelings? Didn't they matter?

She peeked at him. Did he kiss the foundry owner's daughter with the same passion with which he'd kissed Nora? The thought made her stomach sour.

Her hands lowered to her lap. "What will you do when the ironworks are rebuilt? Are you planning to return or stay with your family?"

Jim kept his needle moving, his eyes on his work as he answered. "Depends..."

She waited for him to continue, but the silence stretched too long. "Depends on what?"

"Just, depends." He still didn't look up.

She stabbed her needle into the skirt she'd been mending. Why wouldn't he answer? Perhaps he didn't care for her as she did him, but couldn't they at least continue the friendship they'd once shared? See-sawing her needle through the fabric, she managed to jab her finger. "Ow." She sucked in a breath and tucked the tip of her finger into her mouth.

Jim's head shot up. "What is it?" His eyes dropped to her mouth and he set his work aside. "Here, let me see." He held his hand out for hers.

Slowly, she withdrew the injured finger from her lips and placed it in his hand.

His calloused fingers wrapped gently around her palm, tugging her closer. He tipped her finger toward the light of the fire. "Just a poke, I think. Seems all right." Still, he didn't release her hand. His thumb traced slow circles on her palm. "Does it hurt much?" His voice was husky, quiet.

"N-no. Not much." She couldn't think straight with him caressing her like that.

"Good." He released her and leaned back into his chair, taking up his sewing again.

While she struggled to regain control of her breathing, he resumed his work like nothing had happened. She scowled. What was wrong with him? How could he touch her like that one minute and then act like she wasn't even there the next? "Does Miss Iverson know you can sew?"

His head shot up again, a scowl on his face. "Who told you about her?"

Then it was true. She struggled to keep the hurt from her expression. Why had she allowed Mrs. Davidson to build her hope? Nora sniffed and picked up the tattered skirt. Taking a careful stitch, she kept her eyes down. "Father has friends in Cleveland. It seems you two have been making quite a spectacle of yourselves." A voice inside warned her to stop, but the anger was stronger. "Did you really come home to rest and recover, or are you running from her, too?"

From the corner of her eye, Nora saw Jim set his sewing aside. "What's that supposed to mean?"

She attempted to take another stitch, but her hands trembled too violently. Tossing the skirt aside, she jumped to her feet. She was through tormenting herself. How could she have been so mistaken in Jim's character? She flung her needle and thread into her basket.

Jim stood and took a step toward her. "What're you doing?"

Her whole body shook—with rage? with grief?—as she lifted the basket and marched toward the front door.

He grabbed her arm, bringing her to a halt. "You didn't answer me." Like his grip, his voice was gentle, but firm.

Jerking her arm free, she stepped away. "Jim Brooks, you are a yellow-bellied snake and I want nothing more to do with you!"

Chapter 12

Henry folded his hands atop his desk, keeping his expression a careful balance between resolve and compassion. "I am sorry, Mr. Aimes, but the bank has determined that in the interests of good business and in light of its obligations to its shareholders and other patrons, it cannot continue to extend credit to you. I'm afraid you'll need to remit the amount owed no later than the first of January or else vacate the land which will thence become property of the bank as its due for monies owed."

Mr. Aimes's shoulders slumped a moment, then he straightened. "I understand." With a proud set to his jaw, the older man stood and stalked from the bank.

Henry fell back against his chair. This was the worst part of his job. It wasn't Mr. Aimes's fault blight had destroyed his crops last spring. Several of the local farmers had suffered similar troubles, but for some reason, Mr. Aimes's farm had suffered more than most. Add to that, two previous years of failed crops and his wife and child dying in labor three months ago and it was a wonder the man found the strength to continue. Yet as much as Henry wished they could grant another extension on the man's loan, it simply wouldn't be financially wise. Mr. Aimes had no assets left with which to guarantee the bank would see a return on its investment should the farmer suffer another loss. Witnessing the struggles and failures of his own family's farm had convinced Henry at a young age that such a risky, labor-intensive life was not for him. He was far better suited to working with his head than with his hands and felt certain he'd find greater success in doing so. Unlike pests, crop disease, and the weather, the inherent risks of the banking industry could be easily managed through the diversification of investments as guided by the wisdom of those with more experience. Which was why he was so grateful Mr. Taylor had taken Henry under his wing. He couldn't have asked for a better mentor.

Henry frowned. Mr. Taylor would have made an excellent father-in-law. Why couldn't Nora see how well-suited they were to each other? Despite his bitter accusation, he knew she was no snob. Which was why her rejection so confused him. With her family's connections, her beauty and intelligence, and the natural acumen Mr. Taylor regularly praised in Henry, they could have built an empire to pass on to their children and their grandchildren. How could she say they didn't match? They were a perfect match. So why had she turned him down? No matter how he looked at the variables, he could not see how their marriage wasn't the obvious choice. It simply didn't add up.

As Henry returned Mr. Aimes's documents to their proper file, Mr. Morton—Millsworth Bank's new manager-in-training—exited Mr. Taylor's office and approached. Henry found a smile for the man. "Hi, Mr. Morton. Is there something I can do for you?"

"Mr. Taylor wishes to speak with you."

Henry glanced toward Mr. Taylor's open office door even though he couldn't see his employer due to the positioning of the man's large desk just to the left of the opening. Although Nora's father generously spent the first half hour of each day instructing and advising Henry in preparation for their transition to Boston, Mr. Taylor rarely spoke with Henry during the bank's business hours. And even their morning sessions had been cut short these past few days. Mr. Taylor had said he was much too busy training Mr. Morton. Which made sense since they were scheduled to leave for Boston in less than four weeks. Still, the timing of it with Nora's rejection left an unease in Henry's gut. He looked back to Mr. Morton. "Did he say what it was about?"

Mr. Morton shook his head. "Nope. Just that he wanted to see you." Message delivered, the manager-in-training returned to his own desk.

Taking a deep breath, Henry rose to his feet and forced them to move one after the other across the room. *You're being silly. He probably just wants to share some bit of news or … or …* For the first time in his life, Henry couldn't conjure another idea. But it didn't matter because by then he stood in Mr. Taylor's open door. He swallowed. "You wanted to see me, sir?"

Mr. Taylor looked up, his grim expression doing nothing to allay the nerves jigging up Henry's spine. "Yes. Come in and close the door, would you?"

Close the door? Henry's gut sank as he followed the instructions.

"Take a seat."

Henry sank onto the edge of the wooden chair, facing his employer across the wide desk. "Is something wrong, sir?"

"I noticed you haven't been by to see Nora these past few days, and when I asked my wife about it this morning, she said you'd given up the pursuit. Is that true?"

Henry let his gaze fall to his lap. "She rejected my proposal, sir."

"I see." Henry glanced up to find a sorrowful expression on Mr. Taylor's face. "I'm very sorry to hear that."

"Yes, sir."

"That's it then? You've given up? After all these months?"

"I don't know what more I can do, sir. I tried…" The rest of his words got stuck in his throat. He'd tried everything. He'd been so patient, shown her in so many different ways how good their union might be. Still, she rejected him. How much rejection should a man take? Henry shrugged.

"Are you certain she rejected you? Completely? Is it possible you misunderstood?"

Henry replayed his conversation with Nora in his mind. *Had* he misunderstood?

"Perhaps she just needs more time, eh? A bit of flattery, perhaps? Have you tried gifts? I know it isn't the usual way of things, but in this case, I'd allow it."

Henry opened his mouth to inform the man of how brutally Nora had rejected Henry's heartfelt gift, but his employer wasn't finished speaking.

"I certainly hope there's been a misunderstanding." Mr. Taylor rested his elbows on the desk, his fingertips pressed together. "I'd hate to see all the time I've invested in you, all the promise of your bright future, gone to waste." He leaned forward. "You do understand that if things are truly over between the two of you, I can't take you with us to Boston?"

Henry felt the words like a blow to the gut.

"How would it look? A former beau of my daughter's traveling with us? To say nothing of my introducing you to my colleagues in Boston. People would naturally assume there was some understanding between you and my daughter. Word would spread and other suitors might be scared off." Mr. Taylor shook his head. "But I'm certain it won't come to that. It's all just a misunderstanding, right, my boy?"

Henry swallowed. Nodded.

"Good, then." Mr. Taylor grinned at him. "Glad to hear it." He waved a dismissive hand. "That is all. You may return to your duties."

Somehow Henry made it back to his desk and lowered himself into the chair. His eyes drifted to the lightly falling snow out the window. *What am I going to do?*

J im's mouth hung wide as the front door slammed behind Nora. He blinked. What on earth had gotten into that woman?

Ma's head poked out of the kitchen. "You going to let her say something like that and walk away?"

His mouth closed. Ma was right.

He strode across the room and jerked the door open.

Nora needed to explain herself.

His eyes scanned the empty yard dusted in a layer of the freshly fallen snow that continued to drift from the sky. Where did she go? A line of small bootprints trailed through the white powder to the barn. She must be fetching her horse. He scowled as he stomped his way to the barn door. If she thought he was going to help her saddle it after the way she'd just spoken to him, she had another think coming. He jerked the door open and stepped into the dim interior.

A gasp sounded from one of the stalls, followed by several sniffs.

He strode to the one that held Nora's Arabian mare and found Nora crouched in the far corner, her back turned to him. Had she dropped something? "What're you doing down there?"

She sniffed again before answering. "Go away."

It was the response he'd expected, but the tone was all wrong. Instead of spitting fire as she'd been in the house, her voice sounded strained, sad, like she was...crying.

Every ounce of fight drained right out of him.

Running a soothing hand along the mare's back, he approached the spot where Nora huddled. He squatted behind her and laid a hand on her back.

With a wail, she whirled and flung herself into his arms, nearly knocking him off-balance. Burying her face in his shirt, she sobbed.

Wrapping his arms around her, he gently stroked her silky brown hair. "Nora, darling, what's wrong?"

"Don't," she whimpered between sobs.

He froze. Did she not like him touching her hair? "Don't what?"

"Don't call me that. You don't mean it."

Don't call her what? Jim searched his memory for what he'd said. With a start he realized an endearment had slipped from his lips. She was right. He had no right to call her such things. "I'm sorry. I wasn't thinking. I won't say it again."

Rather than soothe her, his words seemed to increase her distress as she let loose a loud moan.

What should he do? The memory of holding her in his arms had tormented him for months. Here he was holding her again, but this wasn't how he'd dreamed it'd be. He never wanted her to hurt like this. What was it that pained her so? He racked his brain but could think of nothing.

Henry would know.

The thought was as welcome as a wet blanket in a blizzard, but he forced himself to speak the words. "Should I get Henry?"

"No!" Nora's arms tightened around him even as she tipped her head back to stare at him. "Don't you understand? I don't want Henry. I want *you*."

"Nora..." Wonder stole his breath as he stared at her red-rimmed eyes, pink nose, and wet cheeks. She was the most beautiful woman he'd ever known. And she wanted *him*?

Before he could gather his wits, she ducked her head and pushed out of his reach. "It's all right." She wiped her face with the backs of her hands as she pressed herself against the wall of the stall. "I know you don't feel the same for me. I—I'm sorry for what I said before."

"Forget about that." He waved his hand like he was swatting a pesky fly. "Why're you crying?"

She tipped her head. "You really don't know?"

A strange idea popped into his mind, but he dismissed it. That couldn't be right. He shook his head.

Her lips tipped sideways in a sad smile. "I love you." She took a deep shuddering breath. "And it hurts that you don't love me back."

That was what was hurting her? "But I do!"

Chapter 13

As Nora's face lit with joy, the reality of what Jim had confessed struck him. "But you shouldn't love me! You're supposed to love Henry. He's the one with the book learning and the bright future. Ma says you turned him down, though. Why would you do that?"

As he spoke, Nora's grin shrank until her lips pinched together. With a gasp she whirled around, grabbed two fistfuls of hay from the feed trough on the wall, and spun back to hurl it in his face. "Because I want to marry you, you block-head!"

Jim held his hands up. "That's just it. I am a block-head. You're not thinking right. Marrying me would be—"

"Crazy as tying bows on a sow?" Nora pulled something from her pocket and held it up.

Jim gaped. It was the ribbon she'd been wearing the day they painted her family's front parlor. It still had the blue paint specks on it. "You kept it."

"Yep." Laughing, she darted from the barn.

Unable to resist, Jim followed her into the yard.

Before he knew what she was about, she climbed into the pigpen and tied a big fat bow around their sow's neck.

Spinning to face him, her wide grin wobbled. "I've always been a little crazy." The grin faded entirely as she climbed out of the pen and came to stand before him. "I'm asking you to love me anyway. To maybe even be a little crazy *with* me." Taking his hands in hers, she leaned close and pushed up on her toes so that their faces were mere inches apart. "Can you be crazy with me, Jim? For the rest of our lives?"

Jim stared at her. The love in her eyes—her expression pleading with him to say yes—was more than he could resist. He squeezed her hands. "If crazy means spending the rest of my life loving you, I went crazy a long time ago." He bent low and pressed his lips to hers with all the tenderness he felt for her.

She wrapped her arms around his neck and pressed her body close enough that he felt the boning of her stays pressing against his chest.

With a groan, he deepened their kiss, pouring every pent-up ounce of his love into it. It wasn't enough. He would never be able to show her how much she meant to him. But he'd spend the rest of his life trying.

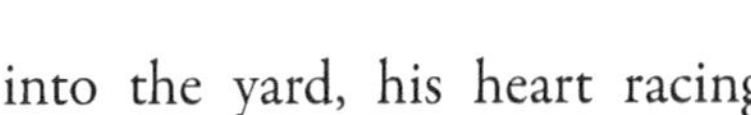

Henry galloped into the yard, his heart racing. He'd ridden straight to the Taylors' house after work, but Nora wasn't at home. When he asked where she was, the butler said Nora was at Henry's house! Instant elation had filled his heart. Nora could have no other reason to visit his home but to confess her change of heart. Everything was going to be well again.

Reining his horse to a halt in front of the house, Henry flung himself from the saddle and strode toward the front door. As he reached for the knob, movement to his left caught his eye. Glancing that way, he froze.

It couldn't be.

He rubbed hard on both eyes. When he opened them again the apparition remained. There, beside the pig corral, stood his older brother—his best friend and protector—kissing the woman Henry loved. Fire grew inside him. How could Jim do this? *How could he ruin my life, everything I've worked for? No!* This wasn't happening!

Clenching his jaw, Henry tore across the yard. Grabbing a fistful of Jim's shirt, he yanked his brother away from Nora and spun him around. "Traitor!" The word ripped from his lips as he pounded his fist into Jim's face with all the fury he could muster.

A sprinkling of blood sprayed the air as Jim staggered backward. Someone screamed.

"How could you?" Henry swung again, landing a blow to Jim's jaw that sent his giant of a brother sprawling into the dirt. "Get up! Get up and fight me like a man!" He kicked dirt into the traitor's face. "How long? How long have you been seeing her behind my back?"

"Stop it!" Nora yanked at his arm. "Stop it! Leave him alone!"

Henry ignored her. It was too much. All the hopes and dreams he'd nurtured, all his patience and heartache—and all along his big brother had been going behind his back, stealing the woman Henry loved. Had he been laughing at Henry's foolishness? He shook off Nora's grip and started pacing in front of Jim. "You've been writing her this whole time, haven't you?"

Ma burst from the house. "What's going on? Henry? Jim? What're you doing? What's happened?"

Jim regained his feet.

He said something to Ma, but a sickening thought bloomed in Henry's mind, deafening him to all else. *No!* But it twisted and churned until he had to fling it free or die of its poison. He grabbed Jim's shirt, dragging him close. "You never came back to visit *us*. Not once. But I bet you sneaked back to see *her*, didn't you?" He slammed his fist into Jim's face again and again. "You—" He let loose words that surely burned Ma's ears, but something inside him had shut off. Nothing mattered anymore. Everything was ruined.

"Henry, stop this at once! Henry!" Ma's voice faded as she picked up her skirts and ran for the fields, screaming "Otis! Otis!"

Henry slammed his fist into the side of Jim's skull. "Or did *she* come to see *you*? How cozy *was* that room you rented in Cleveland?"

An enraged cry sounded behind him just before something struck the back of his head.

Chapter 14

"Jim!" Nora let the heavy board fall to the ground as Jim—finally free from his brother's grip—staggered backward into the fencing of the pigpen, coughs rattling his body. "Oh darling, look at you!" Her vision blurred with tears as she grasped his hands. "Come on, we need to get you into the house. You need to sit down. I'll clean you up and—"

Jim tried to speak but his words were mangled by coughs.

"Don't speak. Just come." She tugged him forward.

He resisted, shaking his head.

"What is it?"

Still coughing uncontrollably, Jim pointed behind her and she turned. *Henry!*

Henry lay prostrate in the dirt where he'd fallen after she clubbed him with the board. "Oh, Henry! Oh, no!" Dropping to her knees, she rolled him onto his back. *Please, God.* Holding her breath, she placed her fingertips at his neck. The delicate beats of his lifeblood pulsed against her touch. *Thank You, Lord.* She hadn't wanted to hurt him. Hadn't been thinking of anything when she swung that board except getting him to stop attacking Jim. Oh, what had she done? These men were brothers and she'd turned them against each other. This was all her fault! "Wake up!" She ran a hand over Henry's forehead, brushing back his hair. "Please, Henry! Wake up!" Grabbing his shoulders, she shook him gently.

He moaned, his face scrunching in pain.

"Thank you, God," she whispered.

Footsteps pounded into the yard. She looked up to see Otis Davidson barreling toward them with Mrs. Davidson not far behind.

"What happened?" The senior Mr. Davidson looked from one son to the other before dropping to the ground beside Henry, across from Nora. "Henry? Can you hear me, boy?"

Henry moaned again, rolling his head as he did so. "Pa?"

"Oh, thank You, Lord!" Mrs. Davidson's cry burst out as she slid to a stop beside them. "Is he all right?"

Henry's eyes fluttered open connecting with Nora's. She watched confusion give way to pain. Then fury entered their dark depths. He turned to his parents. "I'm all right. Help me up."

Nora returned to Jim's side as Otis helped his youngest son to his feet.

Jim's coughing had subsided. His shoulders were stiff as he watched his little brother rise.

Henry swayed a little before Otis laid a steadying hand on his shoulder. "Take it easy, now."

Henry's eyes swung to Jim's—hatred radiating from his glare. He lunged toward Jim.

Otis grabbed his arm. "Oh no. There's been enough of that." He turned Henry back toward the house, Mrs. Davidson on their son's other side. "You're going inside now to wash up and explain to me why you just scared the life out of your ma." As they led Henry away, Otis called over his shoulder, "You, too, Jim. Let's go."

Nora turned toward the barn. She'd done more than enough damage. It was time for her to go.

Jim snagged her wrist. "Where're you going?" He tugged her till she turned to face him.

She couldn't meet his eyes. "I shouldn't be here. Look what I've done. I—"

"This ain't your fault." He cupped her cheek, lifting it until their gazes met. "Don't go taking this on your tiny shoulders. Leave the blame where it belongs. My shoulders are big enough to handle it."

"But how is this your fault? I'm the one who—"

"I'm the one who didn't have the courage to grasp the treasure I saw in you long before Henry declared his intentions." Jim's shoulders sagged. "If I had, none of this would have happened."

"But if you thought I was treasure so long ago...why didn't you say something?"

Jim rubbed a hand over his face. "I was scared."

"Of me?"

"Of reaching for you and being laughed at. Of claiming you as mine only to have you someday resent me." Jim searched her gaze. "I can't give you none of the things Henry can. You know that, don't you?"

She tipped her head. Silly man. "Will you give me your heart?"

With a groan, he leaned down until their foreheads met. "You already have it."

Oh so carefully, she pressed her lips to the corner of his swollen mouth before drawing back to smile at him. "That's all I need."

Two hours later, Nora led Jim through the front door of her home. Bertram greeted them, his brows raising at the sight of their clasped hands.

"Is Father home, Bertram?"

"Yes, miss. He's in his study."

"And Mother?" Nora prayed her mother wasn't abed with another of her headaches.

"In the parlor."

"Good. Will you ask Father to meet us in the parlor, please? Tell him it's important, but don't tell him that Jim is with me." She wanted a chance to speak before Father worked up a head of steam.

Bertram nodded and turned down the hall.

Nora stepped toward the parlor, but Jim didn't follow. Their arms dangled between them, hands still clasped. "Maybe we should—"

"No." Nora cut off the suggestion, wishing she could as easily stop the fear creeping back into his eyes. Before he could speak again, she tugged him toward the parlor and pulled open the door.

Mother glanced up from her place on the settee as they entered. Her eyes narrowed as she spotted their hands. "Unhand my daughter, Mr. Brooks."

Jim immediately released her, but Nora snatched back his hand.

"Nora, what is the meaning of this? You know it isn't proper for—"

"It's perfectly proper for a betrothed couple to hold hands in the young woman's home, Mother."

"Betrothed!" Mother's hands fluttered to her chest. "Have you lost your senses?"

"Mother!"

"No!" Mother surged to her feet. "Henry, I was willing to consider. Though he has no connections, at least he has some hope for a future with your father's assistance. But him..." Her upper lip curled in a disgusted sneer that conveyed a revulsion she'd have reprimanded Nora for displaying. "And what's wrong with his face?" Her eyes narrowed on Jim. "I understand your family lives on meager means, but I'd at least believed you above fighting for money."

"Mother! Jim has *not* been boxing!"

"Then explain that." Mother pointed to Jim's swollen black eye.

"Henry saw us kissing and—"

"He saw you *what?*" Mother's face grew an alarming shade of red.

From the corner of her eye, she saw Jim wince. She tugged him closer to her side. "Jim is wonderful and I love him. I—"

"But he's a loggerhead!"

"He's no such thing! He—"

"Has no education, no ambition, and certainly no connections." Nora wasn't sure how, but her mother's already perfect posture managed to straighten further. "Absolutely not! I forbid you to throw your future away on this...this...farmer." Mother spat the word like saying it put the taste of foul earth in her mouth.

Jim felt Mrs. Taylor's words as a physical blow.

She stepped toward her daughter, hands out, pleading. "You can't truly wish to be a farmer's wife. Have you even considered what such a life would mean for you? All those hours you spend reading would be sacrificed to the demands of running your own household. You'd have no servants to assist you."

Beside him, Nora's shoulders squared. "Of course I've—"

Ignoring her daughter, Mrs. Taylor turned her glare on Jim. "Does your family even own any books?"

Jim straightened his shoulders. "Yes, ma'am."

"How many?"

Jim had to think on it a moment. Counting Mama's Bible, *The Old Farmer's Almanac* and Henry's stack of—

"And don't include anything Henry will be taking with him when he moves out."

Jim's shoulders sagged. "Three, ma'am."

She raised a skeptical brow. "And those would be?"

"The Bible, *The Old Farmer's Almanac*, and *Gulliver's Travels*." The adventure story had been Henry's Christmas gift to Jim a few years back. Jim had yet to read it.

Mrs. Taylor returned her attention to her daughter. "And you think you will be happy in such a home? You adore your father's library."

"But I do not need it to be happy. No book in the world makes me as happy as being with Jim."

Her mother spun away, then paced back again. "If you will not reconsider for yourself, then think of your children. My grandchildren. Are you willing to deprive them of the comfortable, happy childhood you were given? Can you, in good conscience, deprive them of the opportunities they might be afforded if you would only consider finding happiness with a man of means?"

"I—"

"She's right." His grip loosened as his chin dropped. What had he been thinking?

Nora tightened her grip on him. "She is not right!"

"You deserve better. Your children deserve better. I—" He couldn't look at her as he stepped away, prying his hand from her grasp. "I was being selfish."

Nora caught his shoulders, stopping his retreat. She placed her hands on either side of his face, forcing him to meet her gaze. "You are intelligent and clever. You're one of the bravest, kindest men I know. You understand things about life, about me, that no one else does. I'm never as happy anywhere else as I am when I'm with you. And *our* children will be blessed to claim *you* as their father."

"But I can't teach them anything."

Her lips quirked in a sad smile. "Now you're sounding crazy. Don't you remember all the things you've taught me?"

Mother sputtered. "How can that be? He's never even attended school and you were the best of your class and…"

Mrs. Taylor continued speaking, but Jim no longer heard her. His mind was too full with the flashes of memory Nora's question had pushed to the surface. Teaching her to set traps, to plant seeds, to swim, to fish, to make music with a bit of grass. He'd taught her to ride astride and how to row a dinghy across the river. He'd taught her how to teach a dog new tricks, how to start a fire, and how to paint the sky on a bit of scrap wood using paints they'd made from things they'd found on the farm.

Nora's thumb running across his cheek drew his attention back to the moment. He was surprised to find his hands hand found their way to her waist. He should move them.

He didn't.

"Don't you see?" She stroked his cheek again. "Where you're weak, I'm strong, and where I'd be lost, you can lead the way. God made us to complement each other."

As he drew her closer, something finally clicked into place. Like a puzzle piece that had been missing, but now the picture was complete. *They* were complete. Together, with God, they made a complete picture.

His gaze fell to her lips and he leaned down.

"What is the meaning of this?"

Jim jerked back as Nora's father strode into the room. Reluctantly, Jim released Nora's waist and took her hand.

"I could hear raised voices from my study, but"—his eyes narrowed on Nora—"surely I misunderstood." His gaze swung to Jim. "I'm sure I misinterpreted what I saw when I entered just now as well. I've placed a lot of trust in you, Brooks. Helped your family more than a few times over the years. I'm certain my generosity isn't being repaid by a betrayal of that trust."

Jim cleared his throat. "Sir, I—"

"She says they're betrothed!" Mrs. Taylor wailed and threw herself onto the settee, clearly relinquishing the battle to her husband.

Mr. Taylor clasped his hands behind his back. The casual posture at odds with the hard lines of his expression. "Explain."

Chapter 15

Jim crossed his arms as Mr. Taylor strode to the mantel before turning back to fire another question at him. "Just how do you intend to provide for my daughter?"

Beside him, Nora opened her mouth, but Jim raised his hand, indicating that she needed to let him handle the conversation. Her mouth closed, even if her tightly clamped lips shouted her desire to speak up.

"Like most men around here, I plan to make my living as a farmer. Farming ain't an easy life, but it provides en—"

"If your farm could provide well enough to support a family, you wouldn't have needed to trap rabbits on my land all these years, nor take on odd jobs like painting my parlor, fixing Widow Hennessey's roof, and toting crates at the mercantile."

Jim nodded. "I appreciate your generosity in letting me trap here, sir. And I understand how it might look like I take those other jobs on out of necessity, but those are just a sort of insurance. To lay something by in case of hard times."

"Like the early frost that killed more than three-quarters of the crops around here four years ago." Mr. Taylor shook his head. "If I hadn't stepped in and convinced my partners to take on more loans, half of this town would have lost their homes, their livelihoods."

"And we're right grateful to you for doing that, sir. But you see, that's why I take on those jobs. I—"

"You're forgetting something, Mr. Brooks."

Jim raised his brow in question.

"I know the total amount in your bank account." He nodded once. "And it isn't near enough to see you through another year like that one. What happens if you get two such years in a row?"

Doubt tried to squeeze its way in, but Jim shut it out. "The good Lord will provide."

Mr. Taylor released a humorless laugh. "Right. Remember what I said about those loans? God didn't provide—I did. I'm the only reason you and all your neighbors still have homes to live in. If you think there's any chance I'm letting you put my little girl's happiness and safety at the mercy of an early frost, or drought, or locusts, or any of the millions of other things that threatens your crops, then you're more witless than I figured."

"He's not—" Nora surged forward, but Jim caught her shoulder.

If the man had no faith in God, there weren't nothing Jim could say to set his mind at ease about his daughter's future. "Have you any other objection to my marrying your daughter, sir?"

Mr. Taylor opened his mouth, then snapped it shut. His eyes drew to the ceiling for several tense seconds before returning to search Jim's. Finally, he sighed. "No. You're hardworking, honest, and kind. And I know you genuinely care for my daughter. I have no doubt you would do your best by her, but I'm afraid that simply isn't enough."

Jim's shoulders sagged. What more could he say?

Nora took hold of Jim's hand. "Father, I love you, and I hope you'll come around to seeing that Jim *is* good enough for me. He's *more* than good enough and I am so grateful to claim his love. I can't imagine living my life without him." Her chin lifted. "I *won't* live my life without him."

Jim stared at her. What was she saying?

"If you refuse to give us your blessing, then we'll get married without it." She tugged on his hand as she stepped toward the door. "Come on, Jim. I need to pack my things."

Nora's mother jumped from the settee, speaking for the first time since her husband had entered the room. "You can't leave! I forbid it!"

Nora paused to look back at her mother. "I love you, too, and I hope you'll come to our wedding, but we *are* getting married."

"Then you'll do so with nothing. Do you understand me?" Nora's father strode past them and positioned himself at the bottom of the stairs. "If you choose to defy me, you'll have none of the things I've worked to provide for you. If you throw your lot in with him, he'll have to be the one to provide for you."

Nora gasped and the tears trailing down her cheeks broke Jim's heart. He took her other hand and turned to face her. "No, honey. This ain't right. They're your family."

She tilted her head side to side wiping her cheeks on her shoulders before zinging him with a look so powerful, so filled with confidence and love, that it took his breath away. "*I'm* not sacrificing them. *They're* sacrificing *me*. They think money and things will make me happy, just like Henry did. But you know me better than that. You know my heart. You are my choice, the man I was made for and who was made for me. If they can't accept that, then they can't accept me."

Oh, how he loved this brave, wise, wonderful woman. Jim couldn't help it. He pulled her close and pressed a fierce kiss to her lips. Forcing himself to keep it brief, he pulled back to whisper against her ear. "I love you more than life itself. And I promise to spend every moment of the rest of our lives showing you how much."

Nora kissed his cheek. "I know you will."

Nora awoke to the sound of the door clicking shut. Blinking her eyes against the dim morning light filtering through the thin curtains, it took a moment for Nora to remember where she was. And why. The pain of her parents' rejection caused an ache in her heart so deep, she pressed a hand to her chest to keep it from cracking. Why couldn't they understand? All her life she'd tried to please them, tried to be the daughter they wanted. But pretty dresses, refined manners, and social status had never truly mattered to her. Behaving the way her mother wanted hadn't been difficult, except on days when the sun shone through the windows beckoning her to come out and explore while Mother insisted she practice her needlepoint or piano playing. Even attending the endless parties, teas, and social events in Boston hadn't been all misery. Yet, neither had any of that felt right or comfortable. It was like she'd been wearing a costume, pretending to be someone she wasn't. Only when Mother's headaches had taken her to bed and Nora had escaped to the fields with Jim had she truly felt free to be herself. Jim had never scolded her for messing her hair or told her girls shouldn't climb trees. He'd dared her to climb faster than he and laughingly stuck bits of grass in her hair when her back was turned. Jim not only knew her, but accepted her, entirely as she was, deep in her core. Why couldn't her parents appreciate that? Why couldn't they understand her and accept her the same way?

Shoving the painful thoughts aside, Nora pushed into a sitting position on the pallet Jim's ma had made for her in Amanda's room. A glance at the empty bed across the way let her know Amanda had dressed and left to begin her morning chores.

Well, she may not be an official part of this family until after the ceremony planned for two weeks from now—assuming the preacher would agree to marry them without her parents' approval—but that was no excuse not to make herself useful. As she dressed, she contemplated the previous night's discussion around the table. Henry had stormed off while she and Jim were at her parents' house and hadn't returned until the wee hours of the morning, so she'd been encouraged to take his place beside Jim at the table. It had been decided that Christmas was the perfect day to hold the ceremony. Otis assured them that the preacher wouldn't object to marrying them without Nora's parents' approval once the situation was explained. Still, Nora was nervous at the prospect of making such a request. Amanda had protested that two weeks wasn't enough time to prepare a proper wedding, but Nora had assured her, small and simple would suit her best.

Especially with her parents not planning to attend.

Nora swallowed a heavy sigh as she exited the bedroom. The sounds of cooking drew her toward the kitchen, but a knock at the front door caused her to turn in that direction instead. About to open the door, she paused. This wasn't her home; it wasn't her place to welcome guests. She glanced back at the kitchen door, relieved to see Jim's ma bustling through.

"Did I hear someone knock, dear?"

Nora nodded.

"Well, don't just stand there," she chided as she removed her apron. "Open the door and see who it is."

Without further delay, Nora drew open the door and froze.

Nora blinked. "Mother?"

Her lips pursed in disapproval, Mother nodded. "Good morning, Nora, Mrs. Davidson. I trust I'm not intruding."

"Not at all." Jim's ma stepped forward and pulled Nora aside to allow Mother to enter.

Nora looked into the yard and spied Bertram at the reins of their family carriage. It was empty.

Father hadn't come.

She shut the door and turned to find Mother standing stiffly in the middle of the room.

Mrs. Davidson gestured to their nicest chair. "Won't you have a seat?"

"Thank you, no." Mother shook her head. "I'm not staying. I've only come to collect my daughter now that she's had the night to come to her senses."

"I'm not—"

"I see." Mrs. Davidson smiled graciously in the face of Mother's rude behavior. "And what is it she's meant to have 'come to her senses' about?"

Mother's mouth flapped open and closed. "Why, the idea of marrying your son, of course."

"I thought you wanted her to marry our son. Isn't that what you told me last month?"

"I *said* that I wouldn't object to her marrying your son and you know very well that I meant Henry, not...not..."

"Not Jim?"

"Exactly."

Mrs. Davidson's eyes took on a strange spark. "So you don't want your daughter to be cherished?"

"Of course I do, but—"

"Then you don't want her marriage to be supported by a loving family?"

"Well, naturally, but—"

"Perhaps you object to Jim's desire to do what's right for your daughter no matter the cost to his own happiness?"

"Don't be ridiculous."

"Then you disapprove of his deep faith in his Creator?"

"Having faith is one thing, but expecting God to bail you out of trouble is entirely different and a farmer's life is nothing but trouble. Especially for women."

Nora stepped forward to join the conversation, but a look from Jim's ma silenced her. She'd learned never to interfere when Mrs. Davidson took on that particular expression, because whatever she was about to say would be so laden with wisdom it could only come from God.

"What makes you the happiest, Miriam?"

Nora blinked at the use of her mother's Christian name. Few people took such liberties with her mother, but for some reason, Mother didn't appear to object.

Her wide eyes blinked several times. "I'm sorry?"

"Can you remember the last time you were filled to bursting with joy?"

"I..." Mother sank onto the previously offered seat, visibly contemplating the question.

Mrs. Davidson took the chair across from Mother. "And I mean true joy. Not the simple satisfaction of a task well done, or the thrill of a new bonnet, but the kind of soul-deep joy that sustains you through life's struggles."

Nora held her breath as she tiptoed toward the settee so as not to distract Mother from her contemplation. She sank onto the worn leather cushion.

Mother shrugged. "I suppose it would be the night Nora was born."

Nora barely stifled a gasp at the revelation that her mother had gone so long without experiencing true joy, but Mrs. Davidson simply nodded.

"Children are a gift from God. He trusts them into our care for a time, to raise and love and nurture until they're ready to make decisions for themselves—to follow their own calling from God."

"But she's not ready, she's just a girl, she..." Mother's voice trailed off as she turned to study Nora.

"Your daughter is a strong, intelligent, caring, confident woman who loves the Lord with all her heart." Mrs. Davidson placed a hand on Mother's, drawing her attention. "You've done a wonderful job raising her, but it's time to let go and trust her to follow His calling on her heart. Even if it doesn't look quite how you thought it would."

Mother's gaze traveled around the room, her disdain evident. "This isn't anything I ever wanted for her."

"Isn't it?" Mrs. Davidson smiled. "Look closer." She pointed to the hide chairs. "My husband built those chairs and Jim caught, skinned, and tanned the hides for them because I mentioned in passing how nice it would be to have another pair of chairs." She pointed to the blue walls. "The paint for these walls is the same hue as your parlor because it came from the same batch. Jim spent his hard-earned money on the extra paint so I could enjoy the color of a summer sky even on dark wintry days." She pointed to her knitting basket. "Otto dyed that yarn special for a pair of mittens I wanted to make to match my newest dress." She pointed to a stack of wood and a large pail beside the hearth. "That wood is split and brought in by Henry every morning before he leaves for work at the bank, along with that pail of water. He does it even though it means dressing twice—once in his farm clothes and again in his banking clothes—just to save me a few extra steps." She turned toward a vase of winterberry holly sprigs. "Jim knows I miss my flowers once the frost comes. So a few years ago he moved a couple of these holly bushes closer to the house and tends them like his crops so that—even in the middle of winter—I always have something bright and colorful to cheer me." She smiled at Mother. "I could continue, but I'm hoping you understand what I'm trying to say."

"I think so." Mother scanned the room again before answering. "Your home is filled with the evidence of people who love you."

"And although my life hasn't been without its challenges, God has never failed me and my family has made sure I didn't miss out on those little things that bring me cheer and make my tasks a mite easier." Mrs. Davidson shrugged. "I may not have fancy dresses or high society teas, but I wouldn't trade any of that for the life of faith, hope, and love I have right here on this farm."

A portion of a verse sprang to Nora's mind and escaped her lips as a whisper. "...if a man would give all the substance of his house for love, it would utterly be condemned."

Mother faced her. "What did you say?"

"It's a verse, from the Song of Solomon, I think." Nora's cheeks warmed. She'd never discussed this particular book of the Bible with her mother. "I think it means that love is too valuable to be bought. Which means that no earthly wealth can be valued higher than love." She scooted to the edge of her seat. "It's what I've been trying to tell you. I am very grateful for the blessings you and Father have given me and I mean no disrespect when I say this, but those things—the things you and Father purchased for me—they've never made me truly happy. It's knowing that you loved me and then learning that the God of all the universe loves me, and now knowing that Jim loves me. Those are the things that bring me true joy."

"But—"

"I understand that marrying Jim means I'll have less books to read, fewer new dresses, and no servants. I understand that I'll have to learn to do work that will callous my hands and darken my complexion. I know there will be days when I'll dread the idea of crawling out of bed to face another day of chores. But I also know that I'll enjoy the satisfaction of knowing that what I do matters—in a real, tangible way. I'll know that my efforts make a difference in the lives of those I love and possibly even in the lives of those around us. I won't go to bed at night wondering if the world would notice if I disappeared—which is how I'd feel married to a man who had everything he wanted, including servants to see to his every need and want. Those kinds of men may appreciate and even love their wives, but that kind of life just isn't for me. I won't be happy paying social calls on people I don't care for simply because the connection might further my husband's career. I tried to like it in Boston, truly I did. But it was so noisy and crowded,

I couldn't sleep, and when I did, all I ever dreamed of was returning to Millsworth—of seeing Jim again."

Mother's shoulders sagged. "I had no idea you've felt this way for so long."

Nora nodded. "I've loved him for years—though he didn't know it—and I've spent hours at Mrs. Davidson's side learning what life is like as a farmer's wife. I haven't made this decision lightly or blindly. Please, Mother." Nora crossed to kneel in front of her mother. "Can't you at least try to understand?"

Chapter 16

December 25, 1833
Millsworth, Ohio

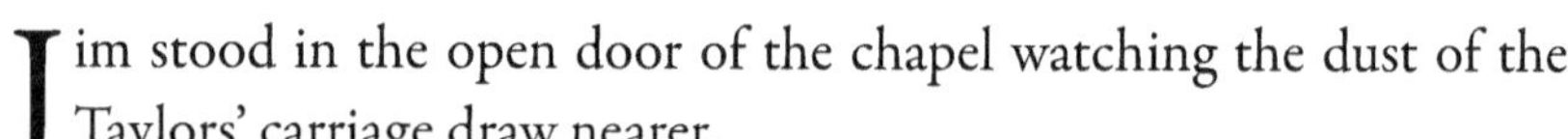

Jim stood in the open door of the chapel watching the dust of the Taylors' carriage draw nearer.

Otis clapped him on the shoulder. "Here she comes. Are you ready?"

Jim turned to face him. "I only wish Henry were here."

Otis winced at the mention of his only offspring. Though he'd loved and raised Jim and Amanda as his own, Henry was the only one of his children who carried his blood. Every member of Jim's family, as well as Nora, had pleaded with Henry to stay in Millsworth, but his younger brother had refused, saying he wouldn't remain "where a traitor was welcomed with open arms." Although, Jim suspected the pain of seeing Nora married to his big brother had more to do with Henry's decision.

All Henry had talked about for years was the raft of opportunities to be found in the large eastern cities. So when he declared his intentions to join a group of fur trappers headed west, no one knew what to think. Ma was beside herself with the fear of what might happen to her baby boy so far from civilization. But not even Ma could dissuade him from leaving. Henry had departed for the frontier the day after Nora's mother had come to visit.

Jim wrapped his arms around his stepfather. "I'm sorry."

Otis patted Jim's back then pushed him away. "None of that, now. He made his choice and Christmas isn't a day for grieving. It's a day for celebrating. Look there." Otis nodded to something in the road behind Jim.

Jim turned as the carriage jangled to a stop in front of the church.

Otis stepped closer, his voice low. "Smile, now. Your bride's arrived."

Jim didn't have to be told. His grin grew of its own accord as Nora, in a cream-colored gown sprigged with holly, peered from the carriage. He rushed forward to assist her.

Otis followed him and assisted a frowning Mrs. Taylor in exiting the carriage. At least she'd come.

Even after Mrs. Taylor had been persuaded to grant her blessing, it had taken several days to persuade Mr. Taylor to give his consent to the marriage and allow his daughter to retrieve her personal belongings.

Jim looked past his bride and her mother to search the carriage's interior.

Empty. Despite her many visits home, Nora'd not been able to persuade her father to attend.

Jim's heart ached for Nora as his eyes sought hers.

A sad moment passed between them and then it was gone, replaced by the joy of beginning their life together.

The pastor came to stand beside Otis. "Ah. Good, we're all here, then. Come on in and let's begin."

Following the pastor, Otis escorted Mrs. Taylor to a seat at the front of the small chapel before taking his place to the right of the pulpit. Jim led Nora to the front of the church where Ma and Amanda waited in their Sunday best.

The ceremony was brief and soon Jim was leading his beloved back up the aisle. When they reached the front stoop, he paused to draw her into his arms and press a gentle kiss to her lips. "I will love you forever, my darling."

"And I, you." Glowing with joy, she stretched up on her toes, lips raised.

He obliged her unspoken request.

———— ❧ ————

September 28, 1834
Millsworth, Ohio

———— ❧ ————

Still panting from exertion, Nora held her arms out.

Her mother-in-law settled the sweet bundle against Nora's chest. "She hasn't opened her eyes yet, but I think all her fingers and toes are where they belong."

Nora smiled as she cuddled her daughter close, the wee one already rooting for nourishment.

Like the ticking of a clock, Jim's pacing in the front room had marked the hours Nora had labored to bring their daughter into the world. The quiet thump of his boots against the wood floor drew nearer. A knock sounded at the bedroom door. "Ma? Nora? Is everything all right?"

Elizabeth grinned at Nora. "Shall I let him in?"

"Yes, please."

Before Elizabeth could reach the door, it swung wide and Jim strode across to the bed, his eyes locked on Nora's. "Are you all right, darling?"

She beamed at him. "I'm wonderful." Shifting the baby girl, Nora raised her so Jim could get a good look. "Meet your daughter."

"She looks just like an angel." Jim's hushed voice was filled with awe as he gazed at their daughter. He pressed his fingertip into her tiny palm and five itty-bitty fingers wrapped around his. "What'll we call her?"

Nora glanced at her mother-in-law already busy tidying the room. "I was thinking of naming her Elizabeth, after your ma."

Elizabeth froze and gaped at her. "What? Oh no, you can't do that."

Jim grinned. "I think that's a fine idea."

Ma waved a rag at them. "No, thank you. I'm honored that you thought of it, but it'll be too confusing having two of us share a name. The Montgomerys have named every one of their boys after their pa and I never am so confused as when I'm trying to figure out if the person speaking is referring to John Jr., John the third, J.M., or Little John."

Nora laughed. "Well, what if I promise to name our next daughter something else?"

Ma frowned. "It'll still be confusing."

"Not if we call her something else for short." Jim paused, his eyes tipping toward the ceiling. "Like maybe Lizzie."

Nora shuddered. "Oh no, that sounds too much like lizard."

Jim nodded. "Okay, what about Eliza, then?"

Nora looked to Elizabeth for approval.

"Well, if you're going to call her Eliza, why not just name her that?"

Nora stared down at her precious blessing. *Eliza Brooks*. Yes. She liked it. "All right." She smiled at Jim just as the tiny bundle let out a squawk that announced she would not be put off from eating much longer. "Eliza Brooks, it is."

Jim settled onto the edge of their bed as Nora nursed their daughter.

Elizabeth moved in and out of the room tidying up.

Nora heard the front door open.

"Everyone all right?" Otis's voice was coated in touching concern.

"Everyone's just fine," Elizabeth said. "Nora's feeding her beautiful baby girl right now."

"A girl?"

"Mm-hm. And they've named her Eliza."

"After you."

Otis was a clever man. Henry had taken after him in that way. She wished he were here to meet his niece. Would they ever see him again?

Eliza squirmed, finished eating. She nuzzled Nora's stomach and drifted to sleep.

Jim slid from the bed. "I'll be right back," he whispered. "I have a surprise for you."

Nora grinned. Jim had been sneaking out to the hayloft each night after dinner for weeks now. She'd suspected he was up to something but hadn't wanted to ruin his plans by asking.

He returned a few minutes later, swinging the door wide with a gentle nudge of his boot. His arms were filled with a beautiful pine wood cradle. As he settled it on the ground beside her, she noticed a carving on the side. Was that...? Trying not to wake Eliza, Nora shifted toward the edge of the bed and tilted to get a better view.

It was. She bit her lips to keep the laughter shaking her shoulders from bursting free and waking their babe.

Jim's eyes sparkled. "Do you like it?"

To her horror, a snort escaped her nose. She clamped a hand over her mouth and peered down at Eliza. How could the babe continue to sleep through the shaking of Nora's mirth?

Elizabeth came into the room then and spotted his gift. "Why Jim, how lov—" Her words cut off, her brow furrowing as she came closer. "Is that a pig on the side? With bows tied round its ears?"

Jim rocked back on his heels, a grin splitting his face. "Yep."

Elizabeth shook her head. "Only a man would be crazy enough to carve pigs onto a cradle. And in ribbons, no less!"

Nora finally swallowed her amusement and caught Jim's eye. "I love it."

Elizabeth laughed. "Then you're both crazy."

Grinning, they replied together, "Crazy as bows on sows."

Epilogue

October, 1850
San Francisco, California

Jim stifled the urge to let loose a long whistle as he stepped up to the front door of the imposing two-story house that matched the address Otis had given him in his final letter before he passed on. He'd urged Jim to seek Henry out, claiming Henry had asked for Jim's address and planned to write to him. That was almost a year ago and no letter from Henry had found Jim in the gold mines. Of course, mail to those areas wasn't exactly reliable and Jim hadn't made a habit of checking for waiting mail at the few places it might be found. He'd been too busy panning for gold.

He glanced at his fifteen-year-old daughter, with her hair chopped short and dressed in oversized, ragged men's clothing. What would Nora think if she could see her daughter now?

Eliza shivered in the rain beside him.

His hollow stomach cramped. He'd been far too busy for much too long. Nora would be ashamed of the way he'd been raising their girl. Was it too late to make it right?

Eliza wiped the rain from her face. "Pa, are you sure this is the right one?"

Unable to speak past the lump in his throat, Jim grunted and knocked on the fancy wood door. He sure hoped Henry stilled lived here. He hoped Otis was right about Henry wanting to make peace. Most of all, Jim prayed Henry would be willing to help.

133

Did you enjoy this book? I hope so!

Would you take a quick minute to leave a review on Goodreads?
I doesn't have to be long. Just a sentence or two sharing what you liked about the story.

Thank you for being a **Kathleen's Readers' Club Member!** I hope you've been enjoying the exclusive content, latest writerly updates, and exclusive giveaways. Your support and encouragement mean a lot as I journey through the writing world. If my writing touches you or you ever have any questions for me, I'd love to hear from you![1]

If you haven't already joined our **Armchair Adventure Krew,** this is your invitation to join the fun! Stop by today and see what's happening![2]

KEEP READING!

---

1. https://kathleendenly.com/contact-me/

2. https://www.facebook.com/groups/ArmchairAdventureKrew/

Want More?

The epilogue you just read was a scene from the first chapter of *Waltz in the Wilderness* which I rewrote in Jim's perspective for this prequel. Here's the description for *Waltz in the Wilderness*[1], Book 1 in the Chaparral Hearts series:

She's desperate to find her missing father. His conscience demands he risk all to help.

Eliza Brooks is haunted by her role in her mother's death, so she'll do anything to find her missing pa—even if it means sneaking aboard a southbound ship. When those meant to protect her abandon and betray her instead, a family friend's unexpected assistance is a blessing she can't refuse. Daniel Clarke came to California to make his fortune, and a stable job as a San Francisco carpenter has earned him more than most have scraped from the local goldfields. But it's been four years since he left Massachusetts and his fiancée is impatient for his return. Bound for home at last, Daniel Clarke finds his heart and plans challenged by a tenacious young woman with haunted eyes. Though every word he utters seems to offend her, he is determined to see her safely returned to her father. Even if that means risking his fragile engagement. When disaster befalls them in the remote wilderness of the Southern California mountains, true feelings are revealed, and both must face heart-rending decisions. But how to decide when every choice before them leads to someone getting hurt?

1. *https://kathleendenly.com/books/waltz-in-the-wilderness/*

Grab your copy of *Waltz in the Wilderness*[2] today at:
https://kathleendenly.com/books/waltz-in-the-wilderness/

---

2. *https://kathleendenly.com/books/waltz-in-the-wilderness/*

About the Author

Kathleen Denly writes historical romance to entertain, encourage, and inspire readers toward a better understanding of our amazing God and how He sees us. She enjoys finding the lesser known pockets of history and bringing them to life through the joys and struggles of her characters.

Sunny California, a favorite setting in her stories, is also her home. She lives there with her loving husband, four young children, two dogs, and nine cats. As a member of the adoption and foster community, children in need are a cause dear to her heart and she finds they make frequent appearances in her stories.

When she isn't writing, researching, or caring for children, she spends her time reading, visiting historical sites, hiking, and crafting.

Kathleen is also a member of **American Christian Fiction Writers** and the award-winning author of the Chaparral Hearts series.

Always happy to hear from her readers, you can **email Kathleen** and follow her on **Facebook, Twitter, Instagram,** and **Pinterest**.